BLANK CANVAS

To @Smiffyjones,

Hope you enjoy the book!

Ta for all the retweets Innit!

FOREWORD

I had this story kicking around in my head for well over two years before it came to page. I wrote the first chapter with some fear as I had decided to write differently to how I always had before. I threw away all the baggage that I normally carry and just wrote, as I wanted to, without asking if others would do it this way or that, if I should be hauling the usual ton of notes and listening to standardised orchestral music and a thousand other questions that normally bubble around my head.

I just wrote and the more I wrote the more I liked what I was writing.

I finished and sent drafts to agents and found test readers that didn't know me personally to look at the book and tell me what they thought, thinking that this would stop anyone telling me they liked it just because they didn't want to offend me. I got back useful comments and observations that I've tried to address in this fully edited version.

I'd like to thank those people that helped me by showing an interest, worded friendly rejection letters, read the first draft and most importantly put up with me staring into space as I tried to work out what I was going to do next instead of eating my dinner.

So, special thanks go to @jomakessix, Mark Lawford and Roderick for the time they took to read the early incarnation of this book and the thought they put into giving me the feedback I needed.

Thanks also must go to the musical artist Martin Harley; his songs accompanied me through the long hours and made them feel whole.

Finally I need to say thank you to my wife Mary who has supported me and encouraged me all the way through the creative process. Thank you and my love will always be with you.

This book was written and edited by E.I.KENDRICK. I hope you enjoy it.

CHAPTERS

1. THE START OF SILENCE 6

2. THE TME OF CHANGE   10

3. MOTIONLESS 14

4. A LOW ROAD TO THE HIGH PEAKS 18

5. THE LOVERS 26

6. STORM BEFORE THE QUIET 30

7. STATE OF THE UNION 38

8. PICKING UP PEANUTS NOW THE PARTIES OVER 48

9. SMILE AND WAVE, SMILE AND WAVE 59

10. FREEDOM 63

11. KING MINOS 73

12. WALLS HAVE SMILES 81

13. A QUESTION UNANSWERED 88

14. A PARTY OF FIVE 95

15. STATUES 104

16. TOUGHEN UP 111

17. ONE DOOR CLOSES AND ANOTHER ONE OPENS 117

18. SALVADOR 123

19. DECK FOURTEEN 143

20. BLESSED 153

21. WHEN THE RAIN COMES 161

22. FATHER'S DARKNESS 173

23. LIGHT 185

24. THE GARDEN 191

25. EPILOGE 195

CHAPTER ONE

THE START OF SILENCE

It is true (at least so in my mind) that the harder the push the more dramatic the recoil, the stronger the force the more defined and obvious the injury or effect. Sometimes we all need a push; an extra incentive to get where we need to go. That goes from getting out of bed to reaching our peak. We can't always do it alone, we need a job and a need for money to take us to vocation, someone to model ourselves on to make us try harder, a prize for us to reach for!

I never wanted to have those things when younger, I just wanted to be able to express how I felt, what I thought and explain how other people's attitudes and actions made me feel. It was, for me, the most obvious and sensible of truths that one can't gain peace with the universe until one is at peace with one's self. How could bringing honour, glory or reward to my family and name mean anything to them if it meant nothing to me?

I motivated myself to seek the truth within and so follow the path of Jesubrahmed; to bring myself to be as God; to be God. I brought myself to the place where the accident happened without fear and confronted the visage of transformation (death) and ultimate change with hope and freedom. What I saw will stop me still in the night and steal my breath in dreams for as long as I have them but I did not quake then, nor do I now. Death holds no horror for me; it does not bring fear, just change and though modern terms like 'transformation' and 'Vessel' describe death and a corpse they are said purely to avoid the obvious event that has occurred.

Forgive me if I continue to remind you of the reality of existence; there is a beginning, a middle, and an end for all things. Death is not something to be sanitised or conversation on it avoided. In a society that chases the mantle of immortality for all death should not have become a taboo. It is an artificially avoidable reality in the present times so I will continue to tell it as straight as my perspective allows, though as a concession to you I will refer to it by its common term, for death is simply a transformation from matter to energy.

When the warning lights flashed I knew I was the nearest to the event and so dropped my bulging, half finished scrambled egg sandwich. Some days I still think of that last indulgent meal and though science tells me I cannot recall the taste purely from memory I know I can feel the texture of the egg, the smell; intense in my nostrils, the warm fresh bread and the taste like an explosion in my mouth. I know I would go back and I know I would finish the sandwich knowing I'd still be the first person there, yet full of that last treat, rather than unsatisfied and sad upon my arrival. Instead I rushed immediately to the core support room; towards the transformation of two crew mates.

That room has not gone, it still hums and thrives deep in the heart of the colony power plant but it will always be where I started my transformation; the one I had waited my whole life to take and yet was unaware of the need to undergo it. In that sense, for me, that room is as changed as I, as transformed as any who witness the ultimate transformation; life to death, animate to inanimate, and so it is gone, replaced by a sense of grandiose and destiny, A romantic veil of importance covering its control boards and screens meaning it is gone as a Core support room and will always be an un-captured space, an anomaly that defies depiction and eludes my artistic eye each time I come to capture it.

Of course Gareth and Lucile will not see the changes or feel the weight or the atmosphere of the room now, they have moved on. In the instant that the coolant gas became critically unbalanced and so vented violently into the room and the lower decks Gareth and Lucile were transformed and so they have no bearing on the location at all, it is left to others to feel their presence or remember their passing. To them the unification happened and they are now no doubt reaping the benefits of a life well lived.

It certainly didn't really matter to them that transformation occurred before they could finish their tryst or that it was I who found their naked bodies propped against the console, still intertwined. Gareth lost none of his enthusiasm for Lucile in their transforming moments as it was so quick that he did not even have time to withdraw himself from her. Instead the freezing gas that blasted the room captured their physical act at the end of what appeared to be a very passionate thrust, beads of frozen sweat covering them like crystals.

Seeing the vent lights indicate that the room was clear of harmful gas did not bring hope to my heart. It was almost certainly their shift time and so I expected to see them there, frozen to their chairs like statues. When the door opened however I found their blue forms pushed together, Lucile's hand pressing down hard on the system flush controls, her arching back pulling her away from Gareth's core in ecstasy, their hips pushed closely together.

Had I finished the sandwich I would probably not have found myself staring into their petrified faces for so long, asking myself why I had not felt such pleasures? Why had I not taken time in the middle of a boring shift to copulate with my co worker, my male unified, my female unified? Why had Lucile looked so ecstatic in his sexual embrace when she had not in mine?

How radiant she looked, how primal and lusting, like a sculpture she seemed to have become the embodiment of passion; of lust. Gareth had also become more than he had ever been before in my eyes and though I had never copulated with him I had wondered on occasion if it would be a pleasurable union. So taught were his frozen muscles; as though he was putting everything he had to offer into this one final act. The concentration etched on his face even made me smile until I looked away and realised that smiling at those recently transformed was of course frowned upon.

Now I look back and can see them so clearly. I can taste the air as I can taste THAT sandwich, feel their ecstasy as easily as I can take air into my lungs or close my eyes, It is a memory so full of colour and taste and smell that it is as much a part of me as my arms or legs, as vital as my heart to my continued being. It is the moment that I started my change, though that is not to say that my change was as easy as opening a door or casting my gaze across frozen naked forms. It would prove a long and hard process which I had prepared for my whole life, even if that preparation was not conscious or planned it gave me the greatest chance of survival in the days to come, and still then the odds were increasing stacked against me.

Even now I think of Gareth and Lucile in their embrace and know they were transformed while looking for God. In my opinion they almost certainly found it, the God in all, in each other, the deity in themselves.

CHAPTER TWO

THE TIME OF CHANGE

I stood, mouth open, leaning in to look closer at Gareth's face, tracking the crystal beads of sweat that were frozen upon his skin. Some had taken enough mass on to have become dislodged from the precipice of his forehead , presumably by his energetic copulating, and had left tracks of lighter blue down the sides of his face. They looked like contour lines on a map, showing the deep gradients of his sexual ecstasy, the peaks and the troughs and I found myself looking down at his chest and then lower towards his genitals. I couldn't see his length or his girth as he was buried inside Lucile up to the very base but it seemed clear to me that he was certainly of suitable proportions to match and satisfy her.

Lucile was young, pretty and athletic as most people were in our 'society of achievement' and in that way we were very much alike, but of course her skin was lighter and she was what many would classify as conventionally attractive (I have less symmetrical features). I'd spent time in the past exploring her body and had found it to be firm and voluptuous, to be full of energy and highly rewarding. She smelt of coolant gas now but when she was alive she loved to smell of strawberries from head to foot. Her hair was brittle and frozen now but it was smooth and floral before and I genuinely look back and remember running my fingers through it while we made love, releasing the smell and delighting in its softness.

As I reminisced and looked closely at their two naked forms I suddenly realized that I had become quite aroused. I blinked and stepped back, confused by the mix of revulsion and excitement that came from being so close to those that had become so uniquely transformed and suddenly worried that I had found myself reaching out to touch Lucile even in this state of Torpor.

I looked sideways, forcing myself back to reality and the truth of the room; that it was a casket for two members of the crew I worked with closely, two people I had considered college and lover for a time and that it was totally inappropriate of me to be so engaged by their transformed nakedness.

My eyes crossed over the controls to make sure all was well again and could see that automated damage control had already started dealing with the lower deck effects of their rampant suicide when they landed on David, who was standing in the doorway watching me. I stayed focused on the wall just behind him for a few seconds before my brain sought out the 'right' (acceptable?) thing to say.

'Captain, Lucile and Gareth have been transformed,' I said quietly. 'They are transformed sir,' I repeated far more clearly.

David watched me and nodded slowly his eyes drifting to the frozen forms perched on and in front of the control panel and then back to me once more.

'They were transformed before I arrived here,' I said quickly, suddenly aware of the implied guilt that came with such a statement; as though telling him I had nothing to do with their transformations would destroy any doubts if he was having them in the first place.

'I know Gita; I checked the damage control and life monitor stations before I came down. I wanted to know what medical equipment I'd need to bring,' he said very clearly, speaking slightly slower than his normal, already measured pace.

'None,' I replied as I allowed myself to look back at them. They were as they had been but a part of my brain almost expected them to collapse in a heap as they had been locked together for so long.

'Are you alright Gita?' He asked me, concern clear in his voice. He genuinely cared for me, as I knew he did, and these people that had so recently been alive and well; Very well by the looks of them.

David walked into the room and put his hand on my shoulder, he squeezed me slightly and I felt his strong arms close around me seconds later in a comforting embrace. I allowed myself to lay my head on his chest, his rough, stubbly chin rested on my forehead. I wrapped my arms around him in return and felt his chest flutter as he gathered his emotions and breathed out slowly. Perhaps this was an un-necessary emotional reaction to a situation as straight forward as the one before us yet I sought comfort anyway.

'I'm sorry David, I know how much keeping people safe means to you,' at first I wasn't sure if I should continue but knew that there really was no turning back now. 'It wasn't your fault that much is clear.'

David nodded and his skin pushed against mine. He was warm and strong and tall. He hadn't started taking the elixir till later in life and so was older in look than most of the people I had met. Perhaps that was part of his appeal? You simply didn't see forty year old men anymore; no one went past thirty at most normally. He stood out at parties and gatherings; anywhere actually. He was in great shape; muscular and well proportioned, handsome but intelligent looking and it was true that he looked every bit how the captain of a special custodial crew should look... only older. He held me in that embrace and I truly felt for him. He wasn't the one pursuing an 'in hours' sexual encounter and didn't get anything out of them transforming yet inevitably it would go on his record. It would see a question mark put against his name and his authority. He simply didn't deserve the position they had put him in. I looked back and resented their selfishness for the first time, though not the last.

'They aren't going anywhere,' David said very clearly, as though he were purposefully keeping his voice strong. 'Let's assess the damage and then clear up here later.'

He hailed the other crew members and he arranged to meet them on the command deck in twenty minutes. We walked slowly there ourselves, checking critical systems on our personal system monitoring pads (or P.S.M.P's for short). All the core electrical and mechanical systems were still working at that point but the engineering section was difficult to access so we decided to follow protocol and avoid the lifts in case of systems failure and so also avoid starving to death in a large rectangular box as it played soothing music.

When we finally reached the bridge I was tired, more drained than I'd been in months, and one look at the rest of our crew mates told us all we needed to know. Something had obviously gone horribly wrong here as well.

CHAPTER THREE

MOTIONLESS

'How bad is the damage?' David asked crossing the room quickly. Ben Stepped forward and held me tight. I kissed him on the lips and hugged him as hard as I could; I wanted to make sure he wasn't going anywhere. I needed to believe he was real, tangible, reliable and alive. He responded with his own bodies need to know I was safe by holding on for dear life. That embrace felt like it went on forever and pushed away all the other thoughts I'd been having, the dark memory of Lucile's naked body intertwined forever with Gareth's, David's strong arms and wizened face and the terrible feeling that the worst was yet to come. When the room went quiet I knew someone had said something of real significance but I hadn't heard it. I needed to know.

'What? I didn't catch that,' I said stepping away from Ben and looking towards Sheena who everyone else was looking at, her red, curly hair rippling down the sides of her face, coming to sit neatly on her shoulders as it always did, the company issued Alice band pulling it away from her features.

'I said I had to cut propulsion to avoid a cascade reaction. '

I looked at her trying to fathom what she was telling me, knowing that I wouldn't like the answer she was about to give my next question.

'But surely that means we are in normal space,' I said quietly.

'Yes, that's correct and no, we can't get back into hyper space as there are no acceleration points in this sector,' she replied. David stepped forward and raised his hands so that all seven of us would know he was about to speak. Even I found it hard not to tell him he wasn't still at school.

'Okay, so you averted a major explosion and saved us all from certain death. Thank you Sheena, but what are you saying? Are you saying we can't get into another gate?' David asked taking another step closer to Sheena.

'I was at my station when the accident happened and saw the coolant build-up. I had no choice but to vent. If I hadn't we all would have gone up!' Sheena took a step backwards and sat down in her chair. She held her head in her hands and then looked up at us all. 'I'm so sorry.'

No-one seemed to know what Sheena was talking about but we all knew it was bad, that she was waiting to tell us the ramifications of her actions on the broader scale and yet could not find the words. Ben stepped round and went to her. He knelt down and hugged Sheena who repeated her last statement quietly. 'I'm so sorry.'

'Sheena? What has happened? Why are you sorry?'

Sheena looked up and at David who seemed to catch hold of what she was intimating and he himself sat down in his chair; the captains chair, plush and leather and situated higher than all the other seats on the bridge; to give him that extra air of importance. He sat there and keyed up his personal system monitoring pad. He scrolled through some screens before landing on the right information, if 'right' is the word I'm looking for (it's probably not).

'Sheena has saved us from a certain death but to be fair we are not out of the woods... Not by a long shot. Now we will need to assess the situation and formulate a plan, check the protocols and make sure everything is covered before we proceed.' David finished and we all looked at him blankly.

'What the fuck does that mean?' Ivan was leaning against one of the many consoles that lined the room. He ran his filthy hand through his hair leaving streaks of grease and oil in his locks and breathed in deeply. He looked like he was in his mid twenties and had a toned, athletic physique. His black hair was cut short but slightly longer than regulation for the ship's doctor, but he didn't really care.

David looked at him and stood up, as he did he looked taller, more focused than before; the doubt that had gathered around him as he sat in that chair forced away with his authority.

'It means we have to run a full diagnostic sweep, each department has to work up a full report and then we have to see if this current mission is recoverable by us or whether we have to move to a rescue standpoint. 'David stepped down from his pedestal. 'Also I have to inform you that Gareth and Lucile were transformed in the accident, when Sheena vented the coolant gas. We have their vessels to remove but it is... A sensitive matter.'

Ivan stood almost completely still as the space between him and David seemed to fill with these heavy words. Sheena wiped a tear away and I found Ben watching me, his eyes searching for something, though for what I have no idea.

'Can I see them? Was it quick?' asked Leon; Lucile's current partner. He stood looking hollow, not falling apart; people accept that Transformation is a part of existence, but still he was visibly diminished by her passing. Leon's brother and fellow astrophysicist, Michael, waited for David's answer and when it didn't come he came to me.

Michael stood before me and his eyes found the answers to his questions as he asked them.

'Was their transformation upsetting or messy?' I indicated they weren't and so he persisted. 'Then it was 'sensitive?' I nodded agreement and he understood with a surprising speed for someone who spends most of his time looking at stars.

'I think you should hang back and let me prepare the bodies Leon. It would be upsetting for you. Can you handle the diagnostic?' Leon looked as though he was about to argue but one look from Ivan put him in his place.

'I will deal with the technical reports and compile Lucile and Gareth's sections too... It'll take my mind of the Transformations. Can I see her before she is placed in stasis?' He scratched his face, down the left side, where the scar crossed from his ear down to his lips, crossing his high, almost feminine cheek bones. He gained it when he fell from his hover bike just prior to the colonies departure leaving him no time to seek out the simple corrective surgery required to remove any trace of the scar.

'Of course, Ivan, you will assist me in the clean up with Gita?' Michael asked as he walked over and embraced his younger sibling. Ivan looked at me and nodded. We had never seen eye to eye and this was not really the sort of situation I ever wanted to be in with him, but I could not refuse, as an eye witness I would have to be told what they would undoubtedly tell Leon instead of the truth. Leon had strong feelings for Lucile, obviously far stronger than hers for him.

As we stood there Ben and David drew closer to discuss with Sheena the diagnostic reports. For me I simply couldn't get those blue figures out of my head. It was all I could see and all I could think about until Michael put his hand on my shoulder and asked me to take them to Lucile and Gareth. I agreed and left David, Ben and Sheena flicking through the diagnostic report assignments. I knew I wouldn't have a diagnostic to perform or reports to file other than my account of the discovery I'd made earlier. I was, after all, simply there to document the trip, provide basic maintenance and clean-up after the others. I have no technical expertise and though I did complete the mandatory basic training in ships systems I am not a scientist.

I am an artist.

CHAPTER FOUR

A LOW ROAD TO THE HIGH PEAKS

I have always felt different from other people, perhaps even segregated. If anything it's been a self imposed state of mind, an alternative reality bubble of my own choosing. It was evident at a young age that I enjoyed playing alone far more than I did with a crowd; other people's rules, games and emotional reactions got in the way of the fun or the intended result of the game, and I hated being told what to do.

This isolated delight of a child would correct her parents from the moment she could talk and make it clear that she found them as difficult to live with as they found her, it wasn't personal just... We didn't fit each other. They were respectful, ordinary and straight forward on the surface; if only in those first years, things changed quickly. They were also very proud of their daughter, whom it was believed would accomplish a great many things indeed.

I was an advanced child, it's true, I walked at eight months , just a few steps, but as they kept telling me I showed 'a higher ability level to all the other children they had met'. I was talking clearly so they could understand me at eighteen months and reading at the age of two and a half years old. This, they would tell people, was a sign of my genius. I have a different take on the matter however.

I remember them showing me cards with pictures of famous people, doing maths in front of me and reading non-stop as they pointed at the letters and words. I remember them playing 'worthy' music to stimulate my brain and showing me only 'educational' material on the screen, mainly natural history programs at first but they soon had me watching hours of early maths and English lessons.

They put up posters of the worlds and asked me to point at different areas of the maps to win sweets. What I really wanted was to be shown some mindless, old fashioned affection. I wanted them to kick a ball with me or play stacking with bricks without spouting crap about the geometric shapes we were using, constantly listing the colours, and counting the sides or the material we were building with. Their desperation for me to succeed built me, honed me, and drove me to do what they didn't want. In short, they taught me to think.

My first word was 'red', not 'mum' or 'dad' or 'dog' as pets were not allowed by my father who believed them to be dirty. I want to tell you that I said it to make them happy, or maybe shut them up from endlessly repeating that damn word but in reality I have no idea what was going through my head. As much as they would tell you I KNEW all of my colours at twelve months that was/is nonsense, I was parroting back to them what they were saying.

I parroted for years, learning what they wanted me too and shined in public for them while I was also known for my misbehaviour and purposeful disruption of their plans. I suppose people would say I didn't want for attention but had they had to solve a maths problem or recite a complicated piece of literature to get a smile from their father? Unlikely.

I was five when the fatal mistake was made. They took me to so many 'educational' places that I don't think I'll ever properly assimilate what I've seen but the one that stuck out was on my birthday when they took their 'genius' to the national art gallery in London. That's where the trouble started. I walked through the halls and sat down in front of the paintings and suddenly realised that the paintings were asking me to think for myself, to search myself and find the answers within my heart. Not only that but my parents were sitting next to me, following me through the grand expansive rooms filled with wonders, not telling me what they meant. It could easily be that they were swept away with the beauty they were seeing but in reality it is far more likely they simply didn't understand what was before them and so said nothing.

The paintings were asking me to feel, they were moving me, creating a change in this small child that my parents could never have predicted.

I am not a sociopath, I function as you do, it's just that I have a greater control over my reactions. I drink in the logical, the information, the data and then process it. My emotional reactions are perhaps slower, more measured than most other peoples but they are there. I'm not cold, though I have been accused of being such; I'm just in control. The reaction, good, bad or different, comes out later, normally through my brush. When I started to push through their indoctrination using the cognitive skills they had taken five years to teach me there were fireworks. I started by spending more time watching rather than actively showing them I was learning. I would think about it for a moment. They surmised that I was just hitting a plateau and that I would push on soon, but of course I had worked out by then what it was I needed to do to get what I wanted. I sat down with them over dinner (we always ate together) and asked them for an easel, a selection of paints, brushes, oils and other supplies, a plain apron to protect my clothes as I hated getting dirty and told them that if they got me these things then I would work harder during the morning so that I could paint in the afternoon. This they loved.

They saw this as negotiation; a complicated give and take barter system that also showed my work ethic by placing work first and play second. They agreed and the next day I repeated, wrote, read and showed them I was learning again. The truth is I hadn't gone through a tough 'education patch' it was simply that they appeared grey to me after the light and colour of the gallery; their smooth young skin hiding old eyes. Anyone that knew this little girl knew that I could do things other people's kids couldn't and so I just started showing them again. I put on a show of it. I pursued my studies and watched them for the pay off and true to their word three days later all the things I'd asked for were in my room. That morning I worked solidly with them and they were full of praise. Come lunch time I prepared my food as always, not because they didn't want too but because they simply didn't do it right.

I then consumed it in record time. They patted me on the head and I disappeared into my room and that was it, they didn't see me again till dinner.

I came out tired, far more tired than I had ever been repeating words or pointing at maps and doing maths. They commentated on how tired I looked and asked whether I was okay? I, of course, replied that I had never ever felt better and was looking forward to work tomorrow. Well this brought them into fits of joy and pride (Oh how they loved my achievements). It was when they took me to bed and saw my paintings that they brought about my first real transformation from girl with an interest to girl on a mission.

My father was cultured but far more interested in the world of computers and statistics. He owned a company that organised and mounted colonising missions and he was very good at his job. His analytical mind (I would argue cold and distant) saw the numbers and wasn't too worried about the human aspect of the missions; it was the mathematical and logistical problems that interested him, not the exploration or adventure. He would go shopping and work out exactly what we needed for the week and buy just that, never compulsively buying because he had already planned for everything. That didn't mean he didn't treat me but it was never spontaneous, never without some price, in extra work or I would have to exchange one thing for another; sugared delights for biscuits, crisps for chocolate.

He looked at my painting's which were all over the room and smiled at them.

'What are they?' He asked with some amusement.

'I wanted to see what they looked like, to see which colours go with each other. I wanted to see how they work,' I replied not understanding his smile, surely it was obvious that these were the beginnings of something great but I could not run before I had learnt to crawl (something else I had done at a very early age; four months I'm told).

'Well, they are very nice pictures,' he replied and his smile widened. I looked at him and couldn't understand why he was mocking me. Why could he not see the birds and the flowers I had painted? Of course I wasn't a master like Scotans from Mars colony yet, what did he want from me?

He read me Jesubrahmed's teachings that night and I was soon asleep but as I drifted off I can clearly remember looking up at him and thinking, 'you know nothing about painting!'

The next morning brought a full on session of education, of insight and of instruction. I put all I could into it but in truth I was even more boring than the day before. This information, these things they needed me to learn meant nothing at all to me. What was the point in knowing how savage our ancestors were? Were they in the room or waiting outside the house to attack us? No, in fact no one was. Our garden was so large that it took me five minutes to walk down to the bottom of it and the wall surrounding the property must have been ten feet high. I have no idea now how big the back garden was in that house as we moved to a bigger one a year later but I think it must have been three hundred yards of unused grass, kept perfectly manicured for the benefit of house guests. The boarders were flowered but it was easy to manage and I'm sure they only hired a gardener so my mother could copulate with him while father browsed figures in the study.

That was the subject of one of my pictures in those first early years. I would normally be indoors reading but since colour had entered my life I had become struck by the urge to see things, touch them, so that I could better capture their image. I wanted to show people what I understood at that point, that as much as a flower is a collection of atoms and molecules and is the shape and colour it is to attract insects (not humans) yet it is also something that affects us. They are gifts, symbols of love and affection, of condolence and grief; they can easily represent transformation in all its complexity. I was in search of the soul of the roses at the bottom of the garden, walking quietly along with my sketch pad when I saw them hidden by the trees. My mother and the gardener, a man like all the others I had seen; in his twenties. He was muscular and obviously strong, much like my father but I realised he was also quiet dirty. His skin was covered in sweat and earth and was shaved of all hair other than on his head. He grunted and pushed against my mother who was being held against the tree, her rose red dress gathered up around her hips and resting on her upper thighs, her back pushing against the bark. She was moaning and smiling and her hands gripped his buttocks to pull him closer as though she never wanted him to be free of her grasp. She was attractive and slim while still retaining what many called 'jaw dropping curves.' The pair of them were engaged in an act that I had been told of but had never witnessed before; they were copulating, and as I had already been told that you needed a license to have more than one child due to the strict population control laws and as we were not eligible I surmised that this was an act of pleasure.

I didn't disturb them but watched for a while and then left when I felt that their act had intensified and my mother had started saying things to him that I knew I should not be hearing ; words I instantly attached to the colour red and its deeper hues; the colour of passion and blood. I walked back to my room and started work on my depiction of the roses, a piece that would bring an impressive reaction from my parents when they saw it four days later.

Dinner was finished and I announced that I had completed my latest work. My mother humoured me (as she always did) by asking to see it. I told them that I had been thinking about how flowers can be used to show emotion and how people feel inside without them having to say it. They nodded their heads and sat on the sofa congratulating each other on how clever their daughter was and what a good job they'd done as I pulled my easel in on wheels.

My father had learnt to be complimentary about my paintings but rarely wanted to see them; instead he would pour through my scientific work or check my creative writing and reading lists. Tonight however he was in a good mood as his company had landed a contract to colonise a particularly harsh world and so was awash with excitement. He smiled as I walked in and picked up his glass, drinking his orange juice and saluting the artist who would become bored of paints soon and pursue a scientific path that would lead myself and him to even greater glory. I never did become bored of it and he would become far less pleased with my efforts as the years went on.

I pulled back the sheet to reveal the image, carefully textured, of two roses locked together in an embrace. The red rose had its stalk wrapped tightly around the black roses and the two flowers met at the top with the black rose dominantly pressing the reds petals aside so that they could grind against each other. The red's top petal curled inwards to envelope the back of the larger black rose and both flowers had droplets of water gathering on their lush, vibrant petals. In the background another large black flower stood alone; facing away, its petals wilting in the darkness in contrast to the entwined roses bathed in glorious sunlight. The background was a dark blue that subtly camouflaged the lonely black rose and emphasised its solitude.

Silence. They didn't move. My father stopped smiling and looked at the painting that was beautifully rendered and was incredibly advanced for a child of six. Mother said nothing but I could see that they both understood instantly, they both knew what I had seen and what I was depicting. They were caught in that moment.

I can remember many feelings, many reactions other people have had to my work but that was one of the most powerful and intimate that I have ever known. I chase that feeling now, that powerful, intoxicating knowledge that someone has seen my work and will never be the same again. This is certainly true of that night as my father looked upon my work and blinked back tears. He walked over to me, knelt down and kissed my forehead as my mother sat silently in her seat, still staring at the painting.

'You are an amazing artist Gita. May I keep this in the front room so that your mother and I can look at it some more while you sleep?'

'Of course you can daddy. I painted it for you,' I replied breathing in his raw emotion, feeling it pouring from him while he spoke so sweetly to me.

'Can you go to bed now? We will have a new and interesting day tomorrow and you look very tired.'

'I am. Goodnight daddy, goodnight mummy.'

I walked off to bed and remember no shouting that night; that was not my father's way I gather. I know that things changed from then on. He hired another house keeper to tidy and clean for us but she was significantly more attractive than the women he had hired before. Soon after that mother hired a handyman who was as strong and active as the gardener and so he hired a cook.

CHAPTER FIVE

THE LOVERS

We stood in the Core Control room looking at the bodies. Michael was obviously upset and angry but I'm sure I saw Ivan smile behind his back. I don't think he was happy about their transformation at all, simply that he saw the absurdity of the circumstance. Michael paced and bit his lip while he thought of the best way to separate them before succumbing to the obvious and asking Ivan for his medical opinion.

Ivan took some time studying them, looking at the bodies and how they were joined and pointed out on more than one occasion that it would be best if they were left intact so that the inevitable investigation would be an open and shut case. Michael explained to him that he thought it best to separate them so that Leon wouldn't have to confront her betrayal but Ivan was quiet and looked at him and studied the bodies and soon Michael accepted that Leon would have to know, even if it would break his heart.

I watched their ballet of words and actions and couldn't help but find the whole thing even more of a farce. How could this be kept quiet? The investigation would reveal that they died copulating and that they had caused as yet unknown damage to the vessel while in the act. They had breached too many company laws not to be noted as being the prime reason for the mission disruption and would never even face any punishment for it. To try and let down Leon was at best pointless and at worst pandering to his fragile psyche.

Michael and Ivan finally agreed after thirty minutes of debate that Leon was to know the truth and that while Michael broke the news to his impressionable younger brother myself and Ivan would take the frozen lovers, fused as they were, and place them in a stasis storage area in the mortuary. Michael left with a heavy heart leaving Ivan and myself alone with the naked vessels.

As Michael's footsteps disappeared down the corridor we looked at each other and then at the copulating statues that had until two hours ago been our co-workers. Ivan was the first to turn away and when I caught him smiling I too broke and felt the need to look away. That set the giggles in motion and we succumbed shamelessly, leaning against the wall opposite the bodies.

'I suppose that could be seen as pretty cold,' he said looking at me. I chuckled and held back my urge to burst out laughing.

'I know. Enough to send a chill down your spine,' I retorted and we were off again.

Down the corridor I heard the Automated Hover Platform approaching to carry the bodies away and snapped out of my strange reaction to the transformed figures before me. Ivan straightened up and shook his head. A few seconds passed and there was his normal face again, tough and chiselled and perhaps as cold as mine?

'It's a bloody stupid way to go but I suppose if you're going out you may as well do it this way,' Ivan remarked as he peered between the bodies looking straight down towards where their genitals were frozen together, 'He's in all the way that's for sure.'

'Could you not defrost them?' I asked smiling slightly.

'No, they are frozen together, any attempt by me to get them apart and bits would start snapping off... And we wouldn't want that.' Ivan operated the control system bringing the tractor beam arm into the room. He fetched the laser scalpel and asked me to press against the two figures to make sure they were properly balanced while he cut them free of the workstation they were frozen too. The gloves he gave me were thick and uncomfortable but they protected me from Gareth's freezing cold skin.

Ivan cut Lucile free from the desk and operated the tractor beam, capturing the two figures and hovering them neatly out onto the platform that was parked in the corridor. Ivan steadied the couple by getting onto the platform and stood behind Lucile, his right hand pushing against her right shoulder and I'm sure I saw him slip his hand round and rest his left on her frozen left breast, though he moved it quickly away when he saw me watching him. For my part I stood behind Gareth and steadied the couple from behind, my left rested on his back while my right drifted down to sit over Lucile's, which was gripping Gareth's buttock roughly.

I would tell you that I found this an unpleasant trip to the mortuary but instead I would describe it as uncomfortable as I found myself becoming more excited with every corridor we traversed. Was it the public nudity or the thought of the necrophilia-like nature of my intimate touching that produced this effect? I think that obviously had a part in it but most of all it was the thought of being caught, or more accurately; how we MUST NOT be caught.

As we stored them I understood why they had chosen to cast off their clothes while on duty and why their passion had been so intense as evident in their solid bodies. The thought of being caught was probably exciting and intoxicating to them. I watched Ivan close the stasis doors and leave them in that frozen, sterile environment and was struck by how much I wanted him to have me. I wanted him to be my gardener with his filthy hands and my lack of real respect or like for him. He was a tool to reach a goal, a taboo, to copulate in front of these two transformed souls.

He turned around and I could see that he was not thinking the same thing. I could see he was regretting the laughter and had arrived at the logical conclusion that I was much darker in construction than he had ever thought.

'Listen, about earlier. I know that laughing was a reaction to the shock and absurdity of the situation, like laughing at a funeral or during a very serious recital,' he said as he started the stasis chamber up and activated the freezing equipment. 'I wouldn't want you to think me unsympathetic or uncaring.'

'No, of course not, I understand Ivan. They were my friends too,' though in truth I was disappointed that he was reacting differently to me now.

'So we can agree not to mention the incident?'

'Of course Ivan, that's the best thing I think.' This of course was a lie and I was let down. How could I still be finding the situation slightly amusing if he wasn't? Was there something wrong with me?

'We'll it's probably time for me to get on with my reports and log the bodies, you should draft your report and then pass it over to the Captain for vetting, we need to make sure it's filled in correctly.'

'Of course,' but I walked out feeling confused again. I knew I was upset, I knew I was excited and I knew that both were probably very common reactions though I wasn't sure the two were meant to mix as headily as they were for me.

Michael broke the news to Leon and he was devastated, I filed my report and Ivan made sure that David checked it so that the investigation would be as straight forward as possible. I tried to dismiss Ivan's patronising insistence that my report be cleared but it annoyed me and I found myself resenting his assumption that I was incapable.

That night the computers ran their checks and gathered the information on the cost to the ship and its crew. I dragged Ben away from his computer as it collected data and we copulated. He was tired and nervous and could tell there was going to be terrible fallout from the day's events. I knew all this as well but it didn't put me off.

CHAPTER SIX

STORM BEFORE THE QUIET

We clocked five hours sleep that night but it brought no balance to the ship, no calm had settled. The quiet of the rooms and corridors was a clever trick, perhaps pulled off by a galaxy renowned illusionist like Jasper Clavich of Mars; a hot bed of talent and still the site of the galaxy's primary indoor entertainment academy.

Clavitch once made the World Host of Titan disappear in front of a packed audience, I witnessed it; I was there. I was sitting in the audience with my mother and the chauffeur Markus; father was on a business trip to Mars at the same time that Clavitch was touring Earth, she had described it as a 'happy exchange'. In truth I always wondered why Markus was employed at all as he could barely drive but I had learnt never to ask why we had hired and fired so many people over the years; it was easier to simply enjoy the new people and not get too attached to them.

Terrance Woogian was a popular entertainer who had recently been appointed as 'The World Host Of Titan,' a sort of ambassador of his trade from Titan to the rest of the universe. He was kicking the show off and it was a big deal to him and a huge vote of confidence. He was a flamboyant man with a loveable, gentle humour, a fantastic singing voice and was known for his ability to get a good interview or performance out of anyone. Anyone on stage with Woogian looked like a God and many had cashed in on this effect later to be found wanting while Woogian continued to deliver long after their star had fallen.

So Titan's new World Host was on stage singing and charming a crowd of Homeworlders in Hyde Park when Clavitch took to the stage by appearing behind Woogian, who made a great display of pretending to be shocked, as though it wasn't planned, like Clavitch wasn't on the posters that claimed it was going to be 'The greatest show ever.' Clavitch was standing before Woogian in his retro suit; all top hat and tails, when my mother reliably informed me that Clavitch was thought to be one of the most attractive and well turned out men in our system; a fact that had obviously not escaped her and not one she would argue with. They bantered and Clavitch pretended to become angry, Woogian made a movement to escape the stage and then he was gone! No puff of smoke or wave of disruption in the air that you may get from a teleporter; he just winked out of existence! In front of a crowd of five thousand people he just vanished. At the time I thought it was remarkable though the later controversy surrounding Clavitch and his attitudes towards sexual partners has tainted that memory and dulled my love of his work.

The stunned crowd watched as Clavitch then continued his act, as though that was just the warm up, and in fairness it was. He made people disappear, read minds, pulled rabbits from hats and even fired a surgical laser cutter through his head with the crowd in awe of his majesty! At the end he asked my mother to join him on stage, she obliged and he paid her the compliments suitable for a woman of her social stature but also spent some time walking the line of taste. He asked if the man in the audience was her husband or 'just her husband of the night?' That brought many a gasp from the audience but he covered himself by claiming there wasn't a man in the galactic rim that wouldn't wish to be by her side. She took all he had to offer with grace and the right amount of humility and pointed out that as he was in 'her park' he should be very careful. Laughter followed and he proceeded to the main event.

She stood still as instructed while Clavitch asked me, 'the princess' as he put it, to say goodbye to my mother, I waved but I wasn't going to be too upset by a trick. Clavitch waved his arms over her body and stepped all around her, he twisted her round three times on the spot until finally she was again facing the front of the audience again, seemingly unmolested. He pulled out a hanky and dropped it in front of her, she bent down to retrieve it for him as requested and disappeared much like Woogian had, the illusionist then stepped to where she had stood and asked if it was true that the old monarchy was really disappearing... Laughter again. He walked across the stage and then spun round and pulled her from thin air near the back of the stage, nowhere near the curtain or sides, a completely void area suddenly full of my voluptuous mother; the queen of The Union of Briton. The crowd erupted into applause as he walked her to the front of the stage again. Clavitch stood beside her and stretched out his arm, took her left earlobe between his index finger and thumb and pulled gently. From the same space my mother occupied came the garishly dressed Woogian looking flushed of face as though he'd been holding his breath for too long.

   The crowd burst to their feet applauding as Clavitch whispered something in my mother's ear as he thanked her for her participation in his act, Woogian bowed and clapped Clavitch off and then played the show out with his most famous song; 'Twice Around The Universe But There Ain't No Beauty But Yours' (he went round twice to check and apparently he's sure).

   We attended the party afterwards and I spoke to Woogian who seemed genuinely pleased to meet me, though I gather that everyone felt that way after a chat with him. I offered to show him some of my paintings and he said he would love to see them. I produced my Infotab and told him to bear in mind that the texture may not come across as well as it does in person.

   He sat with me for ten minutes discussing my art and gave me the impression that he believed that I was 'truly gifted'. When he was called away he got up to leave and then knelt down to talk to me privately.

'Little Gita, never let anyone take your dreams away from you,' he was holding my small hands in his and I could feel the rough skin of his fingers pressing gently into my palms. 'We have so much time now to live that people will tell you that you must use it to live, not study and then others that tell you to study so you may live. If you follow your heart you are doing all that you can and all that you were meant to.' His voice was even and yet enchanting. There was no question in my mind as to whether or not he spoke the truth.

'Your paintings must be seen to be appreciated and they will be appreciated believe me, you have a gift, if you hear it calling you then follow it.'

I nodded at him, a girl of nine standing before the towering Woogian and nodded. He walked away and I could see him mingle with the other guests, each person he came to smiled and he brought cheer to every conversation. This man would help me to realise my dreams later but would also bring about the beginning of a time of great sorrow for me personally. He must share no real blame in what happened as he was just the person that made the introduction, and could not have known what he would be leading me into, and yet it did indeed start with his introduction.

I remember when he was asked later what he thought about what happened between Salvador and I, he replied that he had never seen a talent eclipse another so obviously and completely before, and that he considered it a privilege to think that he had seen me when aged just nine and forming what was clearly the greatest artistic talent of the modern age; but even more importantly he had recognised that I would become a towering force even at that age.

Saying all that I still cannot bring myself to watch his vids; he is associated too closely with Salvador in my memory.

Markus took me home that night while mother stayed at the party as an official guest of Jasper Clavitch's. The chauffer was in a terrible mood and knew as well as I did that she would not be returning home that night and would certainly not be sleeping alone. Even so Markus treated me with care, delivering me to the pretty nanny who helped me get ready for bed and then she saw me safely to sleep with a story of my choosing. When father was home he would read me a serious classic to stimulate my brain and make sure I was fully crammed with knowledge and culture, but when he was away or busy the nanny would read me anything I liked. They read me stories about talking dogs or naughty dragons or playful creatures that lived on asteroids; full of pictures of silly characters and I would laugh. That night I laughed with the nanny for a long time before finally she slipped away and I slept deeply.

I thought of that night, of the promise, the laughter, and the wonder as Ben and I walked towards the bridge, him holding his P.S.M.P full of reports and me with the beverages (as it was my job to see the real experts on the custodial crew were well oiled). We walked through the door to find Sheena and David looking through technical information on the main screen. I handed them their drinks and moved to the side of the room to be 'out of the way; the best place for me,' as Ivan was very fond of saying.

David and Sheena pulled up schematics and Ben added his reports to theirs with layers of damage appearing throughout the ship, nothing obvious, no explosions, all internal damage to systems behind walls; computer networks, air filtration centres, environmental controls; it seemed there wasn't a system Lucile and Gareth's activity hadn't penetrated in some way.

Leon and Michael joined us next, the former looking pale and sickly; he had bags under his eyes and had almost certainly been crying. I watched Michael check to see if he was okay before walking the drinks over to them. Michael thanked me but Leon didn't look up, he took the drink and placed it behind him without sipping from it, 'suit yourself' I thought as I walked back to my corner slightly irritated. Unions end and new ones begin, what was the point in being so emotional about it all?

Michael inputted his and Leon's reports and then withdrew again sheepishly, I could see there was about to be fireworks but I think the others were too close to the screens to really see the look on Michael's face when he walked away from them. David keyed it all onto the screen and we watched the main monitor flash into life, more lines of damage and system corruption ran through the ship adding yet more colour making the schematic look almost cheerful with its lines of primary colours and flashing red 'system fail 'areas.

I suppose I should explain how it looked; after all you may have never been on a colony vessel before. The ship is massive, that's the first thing I need to impress upon you. It carries in its bowels all the supplies that the colony will need to set up their first settlement, including tools, schematics for the prefabricated houses that were to be made from the ship's hull, materials that may take some time to mine or manufacture on arrival including metals and plastics. Finally we have the colonists, who will number between one hundred thousand for a small colony, going anywhere up to a million people for a large one.

Our vessel was called 'The Buckingham' and it was ten miles long, four miles wide and is roughly cylindrical. We had five hundred thousand people; four hundred and eighty thousand of them in full hibernation and twenty thousand in 'partial' making it a very well run affair. All of these 'sleepers' were from the Union of Briton, originally from Homeworld, and made up a significant investment by that state. Mining asteroids and diamond clusters for many years to gather the right resources needed to bring the mission almost assured success was no easy feat. The ones in full hibernation for the whole trip were oblivious of the preparation around them while those in 'partial' were locked into a neural net, allowing them to communicate and plan as a collective, to draw up strategies and work rota's while their bodies rested.

The 'partial's' would awaken on the other side with the plans for first settlements, landing areas, shift rotations, building specs, and food distribution centres. Everyone agrees what job they fulfil as well as their building duties before they leave so each and every Colonist is organised, supplied and accounted for before they even land. These twenty thousand minds form a neural council that make all colony decisions for the first six months, after that time the basic settlements are in place and they then move to a process of elections to find the long term colony leader and his support staff.

Guiding the ship without incident (though not in this case) is the custodial crew; that was us. We stay awake for the three year passage time maintaining systems and making sure we remain on course. When we get within three months of arrival the twenty thousand 'Partials' wake and prepare the ship for landing. As soon as they wake they gather together and know exactly what to do as they have planned it all while their bodies rested.

Every wall, floor plate, piece of glass or mesh, button, door and toilet brush is accounted for on the ship and they are all spoken for. The walls are made of a programmable Graphene-plastics that are hundreds of times stronger than steel and can become transparent or change colour depending on what current you run through it. They are all on a giant grid system on the ship allowing the 'partials' to awaken and create massive spaces for people to operate and sleep in and over the three months that they have before arrival they carve the internal section of the ship into the raw building materials they needed for construct on the planet.

They completely change the guts of the ship leaving only the engine which they will remove on arrival and use as a power supply for the first large settlement. Everything on the Buckingham was owned and to be used by the colonists, bar the custodial crews vessel, which would see the colony settled and spend six months with them before taking the custodial crew home to their giant pay package.

Throughout the custodial period the walls stay grey and boring and must be left in position so that everything is ready for the 'partials' and their preparatory efforts. We, the custodians, must keep it clean, tidy and make sure all is well; something we had done very well up until this point.

Due to the rigid nature of the contract the walls were grey on the bridge as they were everywhere. The touch screens and personal monitoring ports were situated all over the ship but concentrated on every inch of wall on the bridge, constantly updating information and confirming that all was within normal operating tolerances. The captain could link the individual screens to create one large one at the front of the room. Right now it stood twenty feet long and ten feet wide, information exploding over every inch of wall. It was pretty but it was also about to deliver some very bad news.

CHAPTER SEVEN

STATE OF THE UNION

David sat in his chair manoeuvring his icon across the screen, highlighting areas and following them around to try and work out why so much damage was caused by the 'stupid and selfish' act that had been committed. I, for one, could entirely see why the deed had been committed and didn't think it stupid or selfish; it would almost certainly go down in history as one of the most expensive attempted orgasms ever, but it wasn't stupid. He followed the lines round and round and finally came to the almost glaringly obvious conclusion that there was a vital piece of data missing. With that heady leap of intuition out of the way Ivan walked in looking serious, carrying an intensity I would almost classify as dangerous.

'We are in serious trouble,' he proclaimed as he keyed in his data access code and downloaded his reports and diagnostics. 'We lost some colonists.'

David watched the display change as a new blue line of damage assessment rushed around the silhouette of the Buckingham, twisting and changing directions. This thin blue line danced into the cryogenic compartments and then out again leaving a flashing red rectangular icon in its wake. We all waited as it continued its course before finally stopping at the point of origin. Sheena and Ben waited for David to click on the offending icon but he didn't, instead he watched Ivan, his jaw so tight it was as if it were wired shut.

'How many?' He managed to ask through his gritted teeth, actively avoiding the screen flashing before him.

'...One Percent,' Ivan replied as he looked towards the brightly coloured screen. 'We were lucky to get away with just that as well, it could have been one hundred times worse had Sheena not killed the engine.'

'That's five thousand people...' David looked pale and I advanced to give him a glass of water to help with the obvious nausea he was suffering from. Myself I felt very little, I knew that they had transformed and that was sad but I thought about the numbers and concluded one percent was tragic, but acceptable, and so I took that information on board and thanked Jesubrahmed that we had not lost more lives.

The room was quiet, frozen like Lucile and Gareth, consumed by the empty vessels in the cryogenic tanks in the depths of The Buckingham. It was as though they were standing watching us. Actually watching the custodian crew was strange due to my unique position; having no authority and so therefore no culpability for the accident. A mixture of regret, loss and possible fiscal penalties influenced their faces, bringing an uneasy quiet to the room.

David watched the screen then looked at everyone in the room in turn and I could see him switch into business mode as he pulled his pale shirt down and straightened his trousers. It was rare that he took real charge; most of the time there really was no need to, but on that day, right at that point, there was, and so he stepped up. He was in great shape and different to all the other crew due to his advanced age. His muscles knotted slightly differently to Ivan's and any other man I'd seen actually. He stood with authority and the lines on his forty-something face made him look even more commanding.

It was this difference in physical appearance that had drawn me to him in those first months on the ship and brought us to union quickly. He was an excellent lover and made me feel safe but there was something so serious about him, something that reminded me of my father and as soon as I had seen the similarity our days of copulating were numbered. We ended our union amicably and I even copulated with him once or twice after that, but it was mainly due to boredom and

I didn't enjoy it anywhere near as much as I had before I'd connected him with my father.

'We are going to go round the room and have all the bad news now, figure out how bad it is and then come to our conclusions. Yes we will discuss how this affects the status of our pay and whether we need to commission defence lawyers upon arrival. Everyone clear?'

All in the room nodded including me and as he pointed to Sheena I gathered up the cups and made another round of drinks while I accessed my Personal System Monitoring Pad and set the bridge cameras to record from all angles so I could capture this moment for painting later. That was after all why I was awake instead of being with the rest of the sleepers.

'Okay, the venting process was set off at precisely the wrong moment. The reason we have shifts in that sector each day is to make sure this sort of thing doesn't happen, saying that I checked the logs and the protocols hadn't been checked in a week. If they had then they would have seen the failsafe system was damaged and that it needed minor repairs. If they'd done their jobs properly from the start then this would never have happened. Clavitch knows what the hell they were doing in there when they should have been working.' Sheena accepted her drink with a nod and even put her hand on my waist to thank me before I stepped away. She looked around the room and her eyes came to rest on Leon who looked mortified. Sheena's eyes widened but she obviously decided that to dwell on the comments with an apology would only make things worse and so moved on.

'The venting interrupted the F.L.D'S (Faster than Light Drive) cycle and sent it into cascade; too much energy was being produced and leapt to dangerous levels almost straight away. With the working back-up system this would have just been diverted to the secondary venting relay but as it was damaged, it wasn't. Luckily I was at my console and managed to shut the cycle down, this dropped us straight out of transition without 'grading down,' which means most of the damage done to the system is going to be in terms of hardware.' Sheena looked around the room to see if everyone got what she was saying and could see we needed some more clarification. She flicked her long red hair out of her face; clearly a sign that she grew up on Mars, so bright was the colour and so full the body of hair. They like to show off there. She took a drink and looked to continue.

'Gita? Got an Orange?' I picked one out of the small fruits from the bowl we kept on the bridge and tossed it to her. She caught it and held up the fruit, juicy and lush as it was having been in perfect freeze until two days ago.

   Sheena turned and threw the orange at the opposite wall as hard as she could, it impacted and being a small Satsuma it bounced off leaving a nasty spray of juice on the wall where the skin had torn with the force of the collision. I pulled a face involuntarily, knowing I would be the one cleaning up the mess. Sheena walked over, mouthed 'Sorry' at me, and picked up the orange. She showed everyone the fruit again, its juice dripping off her fingers, the skin ripped in places but still largely intact.

'The Gravity generators held us in place so that we didn't all fly into the walls but the systems couldn't take the strain and that's why the damage is so wide spread.' Sheena sat down and tapped her monitor screen highlighting the engine.

'This damage cannot be repaired here; we need a specific tech crew and a support vessel. As of yesterday this ship is dead in space. We have food, drink, power enough to keep us alive and the ship doing what it needs to but no thrust. 'Sheena pulled the screen back from Engineering and set it to highlight other damaged areas of the ship.

'Now the good news is that though the damage cannot be fixed now it's not hard to set right and could be easily covered by the emergency fund meaning that we have not lost our wage on this gig yet. With a quick turnaround at Homeworld docks we can have this mission back on track in no time.'

David shifted on the spot and then sat down to be closer to his access pad. He pulled the view out to show the 'Buckingham' in all its damaged glory and looked disbelievingly at Sheena.

'So this to me says that our ship is very badly damaged but you think it's a quick fix?' He asked as everyone watched Sheena closely.

'I know it looks bad but in reality it could be far worse and most of this damage is systems failure due to hardware malfunction; i.e. replaceable parts like slot in boards. Really, this is not a bad wreck. It takes far less time to replace physical components compared to say having to re-compute the whole route once more or how about inputting the F.L.D 'twist points' in our journey from the very start? '

'Okay Sheena, thank you. Leon and Michael?' David turned his attention to the two brothers. Leon sat down and looked uncomfortable as Michael keyed in his P.S.M.P and highlighted the astrophysics bay located in the upper front section of the ship.

'Right, there is some good news and some bad news. The good news is that there are no strong gravity wells in the area, no big planets and no black holes or other singularities. That means that our drift will be nominal in the grand scale of things and it will be no problem to pick up The Buckingham's signal out here when people come looking for it. That's good.'

David and Sheena nodded and Ivan conceded agreement with a sideways glance. Ben and I stood watching the senior members of the crew. He was becoming more and more tense with every sentence, I could feel him shifting slightly on the spot and when he took my hand in his I nearly cried out in pain as he squeezed it tightly.

'The emergency craft has all the stellar input data in place and has been updated. With its F.L.D at full power and none of the storage and cargo issues of the Buckingham we can travel at ten times the speed we were doing in this crate and with a swift support vessel keeping pace we could be there and back in relatively no time.'

David nodded and called up a stellar map to illustrate our current position as Michael continued.

'We are over half way through the journey, but not by much so, if anything we are lucky it happened now rather than in six months or so. Also The Buckingham is not under any threat from stellar bodies or in any known collision orbits or paths so it could sit here for a prolonged period of time without any pressing need to move it.'

'How long?' Asked Ivan off hand, Michael looked at him irritably but obliged an answer. 'Maybe ten thousand years? Probably a lot longer, twenty, one hundred... Maybe a million if...'

'That's enough Michael thank you!' David interjected hurriedly as Sheena looked more and more disturbed by Michael's answer. Ivan shrugged and Michael sat down looking guilty, I saw him exchange glances with Ben and then look away quickly. I took a look at Ben to see he was very pale and sweat was gathering on his brow even though the room wasn't very hot. I checked everyone else and could see they were becoming increasingly more nervous and so decided enough was enough.

'Listen,' I said clearly, I did not feel afraid and so I carried no fear in my voice. 'I know where this is going so please stop being weird about it.'

They all looked at me and I did my best to smile genuinely. I'm not someone who smiles often, or cries or frowns; I prefer to be level and in control.

'Okay, so if Michael and Leon are done then its Ivan's go,' said David calmly and Ivan nodded and plugged in his P.S.M.P .

'We saw the cascade reaction burn out some cryogenic generators so we lost the one percent. Luckily that one percent is not what we would call vital as they came from the 'stock' cubes rather the organisational section. That's just Cryogenic manifest classifications, I don't see any of these people as 'stock',' said Ivan as he pointed to the burned out power units.

'Obviously with the colonists organised into cubes it does mean they lost a small amount of partial sleepers but I checked the manifest and it wasn't anyone of series note like a council member, so vital plans and services need not be effected.' I listened, finding it interesting how people classified which members of society as 'noteworthy'. I didn't chastise Ivan for his choice of words, nor would I now.

   Protocol dictates that any area compromised in such a way should be locked and be purged so this morning I got David's agreement as necessary and then froze the whole section. The bodies we can sort and prepare respectfully on arrival at colony.'

'How is the uplink feed?' Asked Sheena while tapping on her monitor.

'The feed is unaffected and so I have already instructed the computer to download the details of the accident/incident to the planning council along with a casualty list and a confirmation of emergency action taken.'

'So we are covered that end and they can adjust plans accordingly?' David asked. Ivan nodded in agreement and so all eyes turned to Ben. David looked at him closely and his face became calm and sympathetic as he watched the pair of us standing. Ben sat down and breathed deeply before delivering his news.

'I've checked the laws and punitive actions that could be taken and it's clear to me that there is no danger of anyone facing fiscal or legal ramifications from the accident. As it stands Lucile and Gareth are the ones left holding the bag and they are both free of dependants and clearly cannot be charged with anything, so most likely ninety percent of their fee with be confiscated by the company leaving ten percent to go to their surviving family members. It's about the cleanest resolution you'll ever see in this field of work.' Ben was a fine speaker and a very good company man. He understood the ramifications a misconduct charge could have on any of the surviving crew, so to start by exonerating all in the room was the most logical path to follow. That was after all why we had drifted together; he was capable of excellent logic as well as empathy.

'However the rules are very clear when it comes to this situation and so though it is obvious that we all know what's going to happen I do have to inform the designated captain that 'The Night-watchman' protocols should be implemented as soon as possible.' Sheena looked round at Ben and pulled a rather unattractive face at him, drawing her chin backwards towards her neck and pursing her lips.

'Night-watchman? That's a bit of a cold way of putting it don't you think?!' She continued to stare at him as Ben shock his head and then addressed her personally.

'What would you like me to do Sheena? Rename the position to make it sound more appealing? Get a grip,' he was annoyed at her and didn't conceal it though I was still slightly bemused as to why they were still carrying on about the job at hand. 'So Ivan I have informed the Captain that he needs to shut down the access to all non essential command codes and you need to serve notice to the council that the feed will be disabled before our departure, bar computer led updates and situation reports of course.' Ivan nodded and looked at me coldly. I have no idea why but I got the impression I was being regarded with distaste. What had I done that had brought this reaction? Nothing to my knowledge, unless he was judging me for laughing at Lucile and Gareth? Surely a crime he was also guilty of.

'So it comes to the captain to formalise the emergency action and confirm his intent to activate the night-watchman protocols, confirm the identity of the night-watchman and order damage report correlation for the computer to allow for plans to be drawn.' Ben finished and looked at David who stood and pulled his shirt down slightly to remove the wrinkles gathered in it whilst he was sitting.

'As custodial captain of this vessel I here-by activate The Night-watchman protocol and instruct all members of the crew to compile damage reports and damage control actions and upload them to emergency shuttle alpha as well as to their P.S.M.P's.'

David cleared his throat and stood very still as he spoke, 'I also confirm that crew member Gita Askari is the night-watchman and that all security measures are to be taken to remove sensitive command codes from her reach.'

I wasn't that worried about the coming months at that point, in truth the 'night-watchman' was a position I was very pleased to gain. When told that I would fulfil that role, as well as custodian cleaner, by the colonies Council leader on Homeworld months ago I took it as a badge of honour; proof of my mental resilience.

In explanation the night-watchman protocol was developed to reduce the chances of harm coming to crew or colonists in the event that the ship became damaged or stranded. The position was created following a high profile case in which a stranded crew killed each other and many colonists. Fail safes were put in place to try to make sure the event was never repeated again.

In the event that the ship becomes incapacitated the crew compile all the information needed to exact repairs on the vessel and then transport that information back to their departure point personally to help in the preparation of the rescue mission, this helps to cut down on any administrative mistakes in the amount of materials needed and removes the possibility that crew members could become aggressive towards each other. One crew member would be left on the vessel to safe guard the ship and make sure someone was on board in case of further complications. That one person would be locked from all major ships functions and would be essentially stranded in solitude till the rescue and repair ship returned and would have only limited access with which to affect the vessel.

When I was applying for the position of 'custodial maintenance officer' I sat a series of tests that would reveal my suitability to the position of night-watchman. It was a standard test and one I excelled in due to my solitary nature, centralized emotive core and my ability to entertain and motivate myself.

I was happy to be appointed the position on ship of 'maintenance officer' (cleaner) as it sat in a separate box to my primary role as ship and colonial artist; the duties were minor and still afforded me plenty of time to document the journey through my art. The Night-watchman position was one I was very unlikely to have to fill but when it was awarded to me I felt proud that I had been selected. Standing on the bridge I really couldn't understand the rest of the crew's reactions. Why were they so worried, So apologetic? This was something I had been selected to do because I was most likely to be able to withstand the long months of isolation, what was there to be sorry about? Would they rather that it was one of them?

Out of everyone I thought Ben had the most sensible reaction even though he himself was strangely affected by it. We all understood what we had signed on for before we left Homeworld hadn't we? What was the point in regretting the accident? I was the one to be left as custodian of The Buckingham and I was fine with the decision, why couldn't they be as well?

By the time that meeting was over I was already planning what to do with my time and how to make sure I remained in control. Out of all the crew I firmly believed I was the best equipped to get the job done and perhaps I was right, we will never know how the others would have done because it was me that was selected to stay on the ship and stay I did, for a very long time.

CHAPTER EIGHT

PICKING UP PEANUTS NOW THE PARTIES OVER

I suppose some people would feel betrayed by the idea of being left behind but the facts could not be argued with, company rules had to be followed, and in truth I really wasn't as bothered as I perhaps should have been. They were leaving me behind and as I looked around the living quarters I knew I could make it. Already my brain was seeing what I would move and where, why I would create the spaces I was going too and what it would look like before I had even gotten started.

Survivors don't panic, they plan. I was certainly a planner and survivor and as Ben apologised again and asked me to forgive him I genuinely lost a bit of interest in him. It was as though I was looking forward to waving them all goodbye so I could get started. Then it hit me, this is how I felt when I disappeared into my room for the first time with me recreational paints, just five years old and stepping into a new world; an undiscovered country.

That night we ate together as a group, two chairs empty but still we ate. I was going to prepare a feast but a quick vote saw us all opt for the quick prep rations so we had what we wanted, everyone lining up in front of the microwave to 'bleep' whatever they desired. Ivan had fish and chips, Michael and Leon a pasta dish (Leon picked at his but didn't consume much at all), David a fish pie and myself and Ben shared a Sheppard's pie. Sheena was from Mars and following type she selected the hottest chilli she could find with a triple helping of Virca Rice.

Vicra rice is a misunderstood thing in my opinion. It was found by captain Mutari Vicra of the Perseus; the first colony to be set up outside of our own system some two hundred years ago. Vicra took his craft down and landed on that planet, its appearance and size so close to

Earths that it ended up being called 'Terra', shattering all expectations of how far we could reach by a stellar mile. His colony worked and toiled and it took them three years before they could be considered established. They suffered from water born viral infections and assault from indigenous carnivores, disease, starvation and hyper allergic reactions to the flora in those first terrible years. They took the local ecosystem and tried to assimilate it in the hope that it would calm down the almost fatal hay fever that they suffered in their first summer. Finally Vicra found the right plants to eat and within weeks transformed the lives of the colonists as not only did consumption of the Vicra plant cure all of their acclimatisation problems but it turned out to be a very powerful Stimulant and aphrodisiac. The colony went from illness, misery and lethargy to a hyper state of action and orgasm. They exported it as soon as they could get the processors up and running and sent a drink, pills and a rice based cook-able form to Homeworld. Vicra is a very rich man today and his colony the poster child that pushes all the rest of us out into the universe.

Vicra rice was embraced most by the people of Mars who loved the extra energy and sex-drive it afforded them. They have the greatest demand for it and it still powers their legendary nightlife but for the real people of Mars, growing up in their domes it was the taste that they fell in love with, a nutty, spicy seed that has the texture of Homeworld's rice. Sheena loved it and I know that it came some way to keeping her from being miserable as she suffered terribly from home sickness.

Sheena's homesickness was something I could never understand; I could see the logic of having a job that took you away if it paid well ,which this one did, but if you missed somewhere so much why would you leave? Take a pay cut and stay by what you love, who you love. No, it wasn't that I didn't understand, I suppose it was that I had never felt homesick and so was perhaps slightly jealous. How she could feel so much for such a wide and expansive place like a whole planet when I couldn't muster a frown when I left my parents home and entered the wider world bothered me slightly.

All through my travels, training, my time with Salvador Iranie, even my unions and the many partners I've copulated with over the last ninety eight years, rarely have I felt anything that I would classify as intense in the department of positive emotional connection. I like Ben and he is comfortable, Lucile was exciting and adventurous, David was interesting and instructive, but in truth I have only loved one of my partners; Victoria, she is the exception and even then that was in the middle of my self-imposed exile from art, and so at a strange and unique phase in my existence.

Perhaps it's a result of my analytical upbringing, or maybe; and far more likely in my mind, it's just that I was born this way. I'm not incapable of love or of strong emotion, it's just that I don't let my emotions control me and so I think I dampen anything before it gets to a level I would classify as 'overpowering'. Watching Sheena gallop down her Vicra rice with such glee perplexed me.

They didn't talk at dinner much, normally the crew would relax afterwards if anyone was in the mood and that was not something I usually stayed in the room for, but that night I did. Leon made his excuses and left straight after we had finished dinner but Michael stayed as did everyone else. We sat and I waited for the conversation to burst forwards but it didn't come. I had heard them chat and laugh together before for hours while I cleaned up (as was my job) yet now it was silent. Why? Could it have been that Lucile and Gareth's transformations had left a residue in the area; Homeworlders used to call them 'Ghosts' before Jesubrahamed had shown them the way. I tried to fathom the answer and as I sunk into myself I looked up to see Ivan smiling at me. It snapped me back to the room and I realised that he was not the only one that was looking at me.

'What?' I asked frowning. Ivan smiled even more widely and then leant forward on his grey sofa, Sheena sitting closely next to him, the effects of the vicra rice clearly taking effect as she brushed against Ivan gently.

'I said I'd always thought you didn't sit in here because you didn't want to or we were somehow beneath you, but that's not it is it? You genuinely feel out of place in a social setting don't you?' Ivan wasn't projecting his voice aggressively or mocking me, I could see that, at least that's what I thought anyway, perhaps he was, I'm still not sure.

'Not really. I like to be alone, I like people of course... But I do find them more complicated and harder to get on with than myself. I've rarely sat in here because this is when I'm busy.' It was a statement, clear and unloaded, stripped of ego or bravado.

'But the dishes are there tomorrow, why not relax?' He retorted sitting back, probably feeling triumphant as he had dragged me out into the light of scrutinised conversation. I took his victory and smiled myself, understanding what he clearly didn't; he didn't understand me at all.

'Why would I put off till tomorrow what I can do today? All my life I have made sure I complete the tasks that were required of me before I gave myself any time, being on this ship or the time of day doesn't change my attitude at all,' Ivan's smile slipped slightly but he managed to keep it none the less as he realised that I wasn't done yet.

'Tonight is my last night with you all for what may prove to be a long time, I thought it would be polite to spend this time with you, then take Ben away and make the most of our final night. You wish to ask me a question, do so Ivan, I will not lie. It's not in my nature.' Ivan's eyes sparkled mischievously as Sheena buried her head in his neck and started to stroke his upper thighs. Perhaps she had overdone it on the rice or perhaps that was the intended effect and so she had got the dose just right?

'Okay Gita, I'd like to ask you this; why are you here? How the hell does a princess find herself cleaning up plates and cooking meals for Custodian crewers?'

'I'm here because I have a wish to be. I wanted to go to the new colony and capture the beauty that will undoubtedly be there. When I applied for the post they asked me to capture the voyage as well as the landings and the life we will lead; I could have spent all day painting and being 'expressive' but I felt that if I was to be a member of this new colony I should pave the way to its foundation properly,' I didn't lose my temper because I wasn't angry. I had always know Ivan disliked something about me and now it seemed clear it was my supposed social standing that was the problem, a problem I could easily put straight.

'I may be a 'princess' by title but in reality that means nothing in this world. I have always found my own money as my father did, always been aware that the title is an ornament for our nation rather than an honour for myself and is still kept simply to show people that past ties are not gone forever, and that the Union of Briton remembers where it came from.' I looked at Ben and then back at Ivan who was starting to look more embarrassed than amused.

'You are both from London and I'm sure you've both visited the palaces and parks many times, you know that any notion of Monarchy being elevated above the normal person or citizen is laughable. We are a statue that commemorates the past, there is little money and no state privileges that come with the lineage anymore. We must make our own way.' I sat closer to Ben, felt his warmth as he put his arm around me, noted his affection as he rested against me. 'I am here because I am an artist, commissioned to work for the new colony. Homeworld law states that when an offspring leaves for the colonies their parents may conceive again, a gift I give my parents willingly though it is not one that they will take. You perceive a sociological elitism that is imposed upon me in your own mind, with no real evidence to back such accusations. Ivan, the one who is threatened by my title is you. '

    Ivan watched me carefully as I spoke and refused to look away, this suited me just fine.

'Now if you want to talk let's talk about your status as a doctor and cryogenic expert, the money it must have taken you to get to this place, to be in this position? You come from a family with money and influence; like mine. You come from a place where your parents obviously had more than enough capital to put you on the path that you now walk. You are privileged Ivan and I mean no offense when I tell you that it is obvious that that is not something you find comfortable.' I gestured to his clothes as he sat opposite me, not with menace but with an air to conversation. I wished to cut away his outer image and the reveal to him that I saw him for what he was and that it gave me no concern.

'You dress down when you have vast amounts of capital, you are dirty but a medical practitioner, always finding something manual, physical and mundane to do to fill your time. Much like myself really. You carry a swagger of defiance but you have not had to fight to get to where you are, all you had to do was try and utilise what was made available to you; money and the training that could be secured by it,' I took a sip of my drink and refilled his on the other side of the table.

'If you were comfortable with whom you were and why you do what you do then you would not need to postulate and pose, you could simply be. There is no-one here who would judge you Ivan, I certainly wouldn't.'

Ivan took up his drink and sat back allowing Sheena's hands to wander over his body, still controlled enough for polite company and yet there was no concealing her intentions for the night, nor was there any need.

'Fine, you have me Princess,' replied Ivan between sips of his drink. 'But let's look at you shall we? Capable of a great many things and yet you clean up after us? Why would you throw away your opportunities for this? Because you have issues with your father? Almost certainly. Is this your way of punishing them for being special? To disappear leaving them in the knowledge that you will aspire to the heights of... This?'

I found Ivan's negative view of my situation as almost amusing and felt compelled to respond, also finding myself asking why I had not done this sooner. A discussion without conflict can be revealing to all, not just the winner and loser. Could I gain insight into Ivan that would help capture him on canvas? I hoped so.

'Why would this be a waste of life? I serve a purpose on this ship as much as anyone does in that I have my job and do it to the best of my ability. I clean and maintain and also capture the life of this vessel through my art; art that I store in the cases provided so that the colony can have a sense of journey and history when it is set up. There will be a place where people can go to see how they got to their new world, and know that if they want, or need to, then they can come and ask me about it and I will tell them.' Ivan blinked and looked confused for a moment and even Sheena and Michael took notice. Michael had spent most of his time still pouring over technical details on his pad until now.

'For the six months you are there sure, but you're not staying on the colony are you?' asked Michael quickly.

'It is to be my home. I am commissioned to be the colony artist and when I prove myself and the colony expands I aim to be world host. I did mention this earlier.'

'But why would you turn your back on Homeworld?' Came Michael's reply. He placed his pad down on the low coffee table and was obviously now fully engaged in the conversation.

'I'm not. I was unified with Homeworld, we were one, but I have made the choice to seek new loves and challenges, capture new sights and witness new wonders.'

'So this is your future now? The Buckingham and the new colony? What about Ben?' Interrupted Ivan, I could see he was genuinely perplexed by my decision and confused by how alien it felt to him.

'Ben is free to stay with me and make his home on the colony or continue on this path that he has found wealth and travel on so far. No one person would persuade me to change my course of destiny, unless that person was myself of course.'

'Ben is not going to settle with you on a colony that's just setting up. It's too hard and there really is no reward in it anymore,' it was a statement Ivan obviously believed in completely, Michael nodded his agreement too.

'That's not true,' interjected Sheena having been pulled out of her Vicra high for a short time. 'The universe is full of surprises with new substances, methods and economies starting every year. Some colonies find themselves something unique and export it, in fact most do if you really think about it and that brings affluence, direction, purpose and renown for many outposts, colonies and for that matter colonists!'

Michael turned to David, who I had been keeping an eye on throughout the debate. He was after all the captain but also a psychologist and my first union on the vessel. If anyone was a good judge of how this was going it was him. So far he had not felt the need to step in and make a point, something that pleased me.

'David, you have been on five colonisation missions, which do you think is better; Homeworld or the new worlds?'

David studied Michael and finished his drink, he held his empty cup out to me and got up so all I had to do was pour from my seat. I admired David less since copulating with him but still I respected his humble attitude and his generally caring nature. It was effortless for him to move so I did not have to because HE did not have to think about doing it; it was second nature to him, and that was why he was captain as much as any experience of past colonies or test results had anointed him.

'I think you will always take yourself wherever you go, be it here, on Homeworld or in space. If you are outrunning a past or avoiding a decision perhaps then you will not be truly happy anywhere,' he said as he took a sip of his drink, hot and sweet. David winked at me as he raised his glass in appreciation, again I was reminded of how good a soul he was.

'Colonists; successful ones, are not just lucky... They have made the decision to take this risk, this chance, and from what I've seen they make the most of it. Even if they are not famous or massively wealthy they have more land, a slower or faster pace depending on what they elected to do on the new world. On the whole I think they are the embodiment of our races need to survive and evolve.' We listened as David spoke and it struck me how quickly we had all come to respect him.

'Homeworld is the place it is now because of the off world colonies, what's home world population down to now? Three billion? Slightly more? That is what has made the difference to homeworld; space and the freedom to travel as we care without fear or restriction. But what brought about this time of peace and growth and prosperity?' His question was directed to the room, slightly too much like a school teacher and so I refused to answer him. Let someone else jump through his hoops.

'The religious strife and the ascension,' replied Michael after only a few seconds. I was glad it wasn't Ivan that had decided to answer and as I looked over I saw that he was mirroring my body language as he allowed Sheena to push against him, much like Ben now cuddled me, only more lustful of course.

'That's right in some part Michael. Through adversity and social upheaval comes an elevation in how we operate as a species. Homeworld is still scarred from the industrial irresponsibility of past generations and, of course, all the wars before the unity and certainly it carries with it a ghost of sadness; but the colonies bring hope. The colonists arrive and there is nothing but the future to carry them onwards; they lack the knowledge of the geological past for where they are, so everything is a learning process. ' He drew breath, Ivan quietly removed Sheena's hand from his lap and placed it back on his leg once more.

'In this way both are equal for both have problems, both have difficulties, and yet both have made the decision to make a brighter future. Which do I prefer, well Michael, I like the space between, right here; because we help people to find their futures and we are free of the scars of the past, unless we continue to carry them and keep them with us.'

'But Ben is not going to settle on a far off colony with you is he?' Ivan dragged the question back to its source and I found myself dreading his answer for a reason that I could not find. If he decided to stay then there would be a great deal of paperwork to organise but I would have a link to my past and so would wherefore be glad if he came to that decision, if he left so much the better for him. Why would his answer to this question bother me either way?! And yet it did.

Ben shifted beside me and I felt his arms loosen their grip; this too worried me, which in turn brought confusion. Why was I having an emotional reaction to such a straight forward question? What was going on?

'I don't know what I'll do and I don't think I need to yet, the colony is still a year away,' replied Ben finally but Ivan wasn't going to let this go. He wanted an answer now, though what he gained by its delivery was beyond me.

'I think you know but you don't want to tell Gita because you don't know what she thinks, mainly because none of us know what she thinks; because she is so emotionally repressed that she couldn't give you a reason to stay with her even if you wanted one.' Ivan smiled and I could see now he was here to cause damage. I'd seen that look on the face of my art master and mentor many times and I suppose many would therefore be intimidated by seeing such a cruel twinkle in an eye cast upon them, but I remembered those wicked lines around his eyes also express regret, pain, and even fear, and so I didn't wince but instead resolved to finish this before it became the verbal bloodbath that Ivan wanted it to become.

'Ivan, I can see that you want to cause some division perhaps, maybe some discomfort to arise between myself and Ben, thought I do not understand why. To avoid you forcing issues that could cause offence I'm going to take Ben away and copulate with him as it is our last night together for some time. I can see Sheena has similar designs upon your person and so I will wish you good night. In truth I do not understand your resentment of me and my presence but if it makes you feel any better I bear you no such ill and do not find you distasteful .' I stood and held onto Bens hands. He followed me to a standing position.

'David, if it is acceptable with you I will complete my cleaning up in the morning?' David nodded his agreement and smiled at me warmly. Michael nodded and waved goodnight as we walked out. Ivan and Sheena retired shortly after us but they were heard arguing loudly in his quarters later; the rumour is that he was not up to her high standards when it comes to sexual partners.

CHAPTER NINE

SMILE AND WAVE, SMILE AND WAVE

We copulated twice that night, Ben and I. The first was a tentative, soft, lessoning of tensions as he felt bad that he did not answer with a concrete 'yes' when pressed by Ivan after dinner. I explained as we lay under the light sheets, not particularly sweaty, that I did not need him to commit to me body and soul and that he should relax about the whole situation. We chatted and in time he did indeed relax and the second time we were far more energetic and animated, sweaty and exhausted by the long days talks and revelations we slipped into our cohabited sleep; the last one I would experience for a long time.

I couldn't and wouldn't tell you that Ben was a master of his or my body, that he fulfilled me in all the ways I needed him to or that we 'were meant to be together.' That is not how we were, though I would say that we fitted together well sexually and that he was at least as interested in me as he was in himself, which is in itself a compliment when compared to some of the men I have copulated with.

If I had to give those two acts of physical pleasure a rating I would say they were 'adequate' and that Ben was at least decent enough to sleep tidily on his side of the bed rather than harassing me all night with semiconscious, lazy hugs or clumsy, half-advances he had no intention of following through with. By the time the morning came I found myself in quite a good mood, after all I was to be presented with the perfect opportunity to fulfil my task for the colony. I was going to paint for them so that when they arrived they could have an understanding of what it was like to take this mammoth journey through space and yet still have the luxury of being able to sleep through it.

Breakfast was taken alone, and yet together; I ate and he watched as Ben was not allowed to consume anything before he entered partial stasis, I even teased him with toast and tea that I knew he could not eat and he responded by smiling along though I knew he wanted to be deep and morose and discuss our 'feelings'. I didn't see the point, he would be drawing up a plan of action to get the mission back on track while his body lay in a torpor state, I would be busy; what did our 'feelings' matter now?

We gathered on the lower section docking bay and when I arrived Sheena was motioning to Ivan with her thumb and index finger held very closely together; presumably to indicate a failing in the length of his reproductive organ. Michael was laughing, it was a strained laugh, but a laugh none the less. As the hours ticked by we prepared the craft and I helped where I could but it became obvious that Leon was still not present.

Had we known that Leon had decided to end his existence and had chosen self transformation in the small room where Lucile had herself transformed I'm sure our banter would have been lessened and we would have been more stayed, even mournful, but we did not know and so the morning was almost pleasant. Early afternoon was when Leon was found hanging from the ceiling grill, luckily it was Ivan that discovered the body and cut him down before Michael could witness the empty vessel, and so he was able to hold the body and weep without having to feel the need to prop up his brothers weight; in case there was still hope of revival when it was clear there was none.

That incident didn't stop their vessel from heading back to Homeworld as planned but it did delay them by some hours. Michael was consoled by Sheena while David and I ran through the survival protocols. He was completing his situation analysis and psyche evaluation on me and concluded that I was more than capable of completing my mission to safe guard the vessel while they organised its repair and the mission's continuation. This left Ben and Ivan to remove the body to the stasis area where Lucile and Gareth were also stored.

Ivan was in a bad mood and Ben returned tipping the same way. We held each other but he seemed frustrated and slightly distant, was this Ben's coping mechanism? I didn't know but I was disappointed that he had chosen that point in time to regret whatever it was he hadn't said to me yet. I was already prepared for his departure and it probably would have been easier for me to have them gone swiftly than it was to deal with all the delays and final goodbyes. Still, I waited by the ship, kissed Ben goodbye and wished them all luck.

The ship they boarded was more of a pod container with a Faster than Light Drive attached to the back. It was a short range vessel really but had been adapted to act as the emergency Custodial support ship and so could get from where we were to where they needed to be without any trouble, in fact they would be travelling significantly faster than they had been for the last eighteen months.

The bay needed to be secured before they could depart into space and so I retreated to the observation deck as they started climbing into their partial stasis tubes. I didn't feel the need to talk to them as they readied for departure but left the com open to hear them all clattering round and complaining about how cramped it felt. As they lay down the pods closed automatically and dumped them straight into stasis so I listened carefully and as the lids descended I heard Ben say something, but I couldn't hear what it was as Ivan decided to talk over him. I know he was speaking to me as I'd heard my name but other than that I couldn't make it out and really, what difference would it make for me to ask him to repeat it as he would be unconscious before my words were out, so I said nothing at all.

I watched their unconventional mushroom shaped vessel drift out into space through the airlock. There was no light here really, we were too far from any sun to be touched by light that illuminate them and so I switched the external lights on only to remember that that system was offline. So I tracked the lights flashing on their vessel, saw them twist away indicating that the 'stalk' section of the ship where they were already sleeping was pointing towards its destination and saw the flash of pale blue light as the engine fired them into the universe away from me.

In that moment I think I felt it, knew that it was not just that I was the only one awake on the Buckingham, but that on a ship of four hundred and ninety five thousand people and five thousand and three empty vessels I was unique, I was the only one truly conscious and living and so by definition; alone.

CHAPTER TEN

FREEDOM

    To understand my frame of mind you have to understand that I have always wanted to be left alone. Not alone forever, of course, but instead just to be left to be who I want to be, do what I want to do, when I want to do it. True, this is not a singular feeling owned and honed by me, many, if not all of us, need time to reflect but others crave the solace of company when they have found the peace they required; I have often felt that I could stay without seeing anyone for a year, so long as there was something to fill the gap that the absence of people had left behind; ideally something to study, understand and ultimately capture on canvas.

    I blinked to clear my sight of the blob of colour that burned itself onto my retainers when the ship blasted off into space. I felt driven to leap into action and set up what would be my home for the foreseeable future, but I knew this was going to take a week to get right at least and then another to make sure supplies and details were perfect, to make certain that I would be able to achieve what I wanted to.

    It was in my nature to need a space to be, an area that I could have complete control over, a kingdom built from my own two hands and so that's what I did. I first studied the schematics and drew up my plans, of course I went to clear the kitchen of debris from the night before and wipe all the tables and chairs, mop the floors and atomised the waste but when I arrived I found that David had done it already and had left a note wishing me luck.

    I had already decided that I would record everything I did from this point in and so had cleared with David that it was safe to draw the power from damaged sections to set the motion detector cameras back on. When the negotiations for the custodial crew were drawn up they opted to have the cameras switched off unless in extreme conditions to allow them some freedom on the ship. It meant we could relax without worrying that the company (in this case the colony financial executive) would be fining us every time we slammed a door and it basically meant people could walk around naked if they wanted without having to request the sensitive moments of their comings and goings to be wiped from the banks upon arrival.

I suppose it may have meant that we would not be in the position we were now in if Lucile and Gareth hadn't felt they could copulate while at work but then so many other things would be lost too, not that I could think of anything I had done that I would not want to be caught doing. We all defecate, fornicate and masturbate, what really was the big deal? Saying that I normally hated being on camera as it had been my father's urge to capture my formative years to show people how clever his daughter was. I had a foot in both camps I suppose, but then that is me, I can see both sides of the story even if I don't agree, empathise or understand them.

The cameras captured me watching the ships lights vanish as well as my mixed reaction to finding the kitchen already clean; somewhere between touched and irritated as it was something thoughtfully done and yet it was a task I was more than prepared to do. They watched me tap away on the computer and for once I didn't mind letting my hair down and allowing it to watch me shower or brush my teeth or draw my plan for the next, dare I say year alone? Perhaps far more? It didn't bring any real fear, just a strange emptiness, as though I was a well to be filled with adventure and loneliness and discovery and that it was worse to be empty than it was to be full. I wanted all to see the struggle of the ship; the stranding of The Buckingham! What would I do to keep myself and the ship alive? Well to start with I took my basic knowledge of the ships systems and put in place all the safeguards that I thought I'd need. Alarms to signify times to check pressure and stasis compartments, alarms to remind me to eat or take sustenance of some kind, and I patched the med bays scanner into my P.S.M.P to monitored myself. Making sure I did not deteriorate physically felt very important.

On the front of activity I booked ten runs around the ship, all different grades with stairs and ramps, some with long corridors others with pipe negotiation for manual dexterity and climbing sections. I decided once every two days would be enough to maintain my body while I worked out a rota of food choices to cover my needs and a snack based plan to make sure I had food to hand. Medical emergency equipment was brought to my quarters to make sure I was covered in case of injury and I also unlocked the well being boxes placed in the emergency section.

The emergency boxes and well being sections of The Buckingham had been brought in as a reaction to a lost colonial ship over a hundred years ago. The 'Osprey' had departed on time and all was looking good until it was hit by a stray piece of debris from an asteroid. The ship was left dead in space much like ours but far worse off in terms of damage and with the emergency shuttle destroyed the custodian crew were forced to try to fix the vessel themselves. They managed to get a message out to Homeworld but received no confirmation as the ship was in such disrepair. With little hope of discovery and no chance of being able to get the ship running the crew of seven turned on each other.

Not that much is known about why they fought or if they were victims of more extreme conditions than I found myself in but the fact was that within two months all but one of the crew members were dead and though it's not conclusive many believe they were all led to their transformation by Chad Williams; the last surviving member of the crew and the Ospreys quartermaster and navigation officer.

Williams probably transformed the crew and then when he found himself alone he slipped into a deep insanity that saw him commit some tragic and horrific acts upon the colonists he was there to care for. In the four months he was on the ship alone he woke nineteen women from stasis and copulated with them against their permission; a rare and terrifying crime in our modern society and then transformed them with his own two hands. He also transformed men he 'did not like the look of,' most of them had lighter skin than him; another rare crime. He lived in such filthy conditions that when the airlocks were opened it produced a sickness amongst the rescue crew that physically manifested itself in involuntary vomiting.

Quartermaster Williams was transformed from a man into a monster due to a lack of mental toughness, bad diet, chemical imbalances in his brain and the sinking doom that he was to die there. In his journal (of it that's legible) he confesses that he had never considered transforming others before but that he had certainly kept his frustration at never ending his own life a secret and hoped to be transformed in an accident or attacked by a wild animal while on the new colony.

After Williams all colonial endeavours were more closely scrutinised as it was clear that Williams was planning to transform all one hundred thousand colonists if he survived that long. He had become 'God' through his power over others existences and didn't cared how many of his 'subjects' he destroyed.

The well being boxes were large; eight feet high and thirty three feet deep. They were filled with items that each custodial crew member had selected from the colonists lists of eligible equipment. The list was huge and each person had their own box so it was a financial commitment to the custodian crew of some size by the colonists financiers and yet no colonist wanted to meet the same fate as those on the Osprey, so they supplied the contents of the boxes without argument.

Most of the things in the boxes were generic as they would not be space to transport them home again from the colony on the custodians converted ship but mine was different. I was to stay on the colony and so they had allowed me to pack it full of my own possessions; something that brought much envy from the colonists as they were only allowed a small box of personal possessions to travel with, so small in fact that it had to fit into their stasis chamber by their feet. The rules were strict too, nothing food or drink related and nothing metal. Of course they had all their histories, games, images of family and such on data carriers plugged into the stasis chamber so they could bring their lives with them, just nothing physical from it above the size of a shoe box.

For me the rules had been relaxed, not because of my supposed social status but because of the unique nature of my role on the Buckingham. I was to chronicle the whole journey and the setting up of the new colony, to capture the awesome glory of the physical geography of our new planet and its new people. This meant I had to stay awake to get the ship there, physically paint and capture the souls of the people that would act as custodians for the journey, document the day to day and capture the spirit of the vast distance we were all travelling. Once there I was to paint the beauty of our new home and send back pieces of art to convince Homeworlders to visit and invest their capitol in our new paradise. I could not be afforded more space in the hold but they bent the rules on the well being boxes in the understanding that I would receive those items on arrival or if there was need to unlock the boxes on route, which there now obviously was.

Many of the boxes would seem empty due to a lack of larger items; after all it was unwise to push for expensive items to fill the containers as extravagant tastes may impact on the chances of a custodial crew member gaining employment later down the line. For me it had been perfect to store some furniture, canvas making material and paints. My container was full of it, what else did I need? All media related entertainment was already stored on the ships memory banks anyway. Why would anyone pay to watch or listen to something that could be traded or uploaded to personal devices? Music and entertainment were on file, images and captured footage were also stored the same way, so it was canvas and paint. Canvas, paint, two comfortable chairs, a bean bag and right at the back a small keep sake from my childhood, something I would give to my child when I had one. I was sure I would at some point, why not, I was as fertile as all the other women; surely one day I would find a man to create a union with that would warrant a child? For that eventuality I'd packed the small easel on wheels that had been my fondest friend in childhood. My father had thought it destroyed, thrown out with some of my other things while I was away but my mother had saved it. It was an act I would thank her for though not many of her other actions were worthy of thanks after I had presented that painting to her and my father when I was six. I suppose she felt betrayed.

Along with the personal box I was given access to the group well being crate. In it were stored the things that the experts thought would help long term stranded crew members from pulling 'A Chad', that included sports equipment to allow one, two or more crew members to play single or group activities, keeping them fit, healthy and more likely sane. Behind all that came the therapeutic equipment like scrunch balls, synthetic touch sensors to keep you from becoming sensory deprived and one hundred and one amazing little gadgets that fulfilled the same sort of morale boosting job but in a myriad of ways. There really was something for everyone in there, even me.

I found a large amount of wool and knitting needles; something tactile that I could craft, something that could grow with my imagination and be useful. That was me all over, I disliked not being useful and the thought of wasting my time was distasteful, if not criminal. I had spent ninety-eight years keeping busy; from learning to drool and crawl to reading technical manuals so I could produce the lighting effect I wanted on the ship so I could paint effectively. I didn't do 'down time' so the knitting was perfect for when I was tired physically or planning my next artistic move.

Right at the back of the container was the locked section that I was given the key to by David that morning. I typed in the ten digit code on the pad and watched the door open. Inside the strip-light flickered into life casting light on the more expensive, exclusive and plain sensitive objects; it amused me to discover what the colony leaders considered to be a 'Sensitive' object.

I stepped through the doorway and looked around the small room; a compartment that made up the final three feet of the container. Inside rows of unmarked boxes sat on the shelves. I pulled one down to reveal that they were the 'sexual health' containers, each box containing different sizes of sex toys that were designed to produce different levels and types of pleasure. I stood playing with those objects for some time, giggling every now and then when they became weirder or just strayed into ridiculous proportions. How some of these devices could even fit inside the normal human body was beyond me and I didn't consider myself to be sexually repressed, in fact I had experimented as much as I felt I should and enjoyed those moments for the most part. Still, some of what I found in the restricted section baffled me... Perhaps I was more sheltered than I'd at first thought?

Right in the corner was something that I knew would be needed at some point, not that I liked admitting it. The sleep dummies were in locked cases and these were what I was really after (though perhaps one or two of the sexual devices may have come along with me in a discrete bag... Not that I had any need to be discrete), they had proven invaluable in other such cases of long term forced isolation and so would both be coming out. Of course there was a male and female model and I had been in unions with both men and women and so it seemed natural to take the pair.

I took them, though I refused to name them as the well being guide instructed, and all the other things I wanted and placed them in my quarters which was a twelve by twelve grey walled room near the kitchen that contained a double bed, some painting supplies and my clothing which was all neatly away in a small cupboard in the far corner. The two sleeping aids were placed on the bed while I stored the other bits and pieces under my bed for later. Looking at the sleepers while in the store revealed that I could adjust their weight, height and density so they could be more muscular or alternatively pillow like depending on what I needed. I'd never slept with someone who wasn't in near peak condition, probably the closest to imperfection was David and even he was in excellent shape for a man with a physical body age of forty or so.

I had dropped their weights to ten kg's each to make it easy to transport them to my room but now I accessed the command protocols and increased their weight to twenty five kgs. I placed them both on the floor, sitting up against the wall and left them there as the alarm went off gently in the room, reminding me that it was dinner time. It wasn't necessary to have the alarm in place yet but I knew it would become so and so started early to form a habit that may help keep me alive later in the journey.

Dinner was simple that first night, just some reheated vacuum packed goods that I cobbled together to make a chilli. It was all easy to prepare and satisfied me as much as it ever had. I tided up, washed the dishes and then went to my room early to make sure I was ready for the day tomorrow.

The night was quiet and I had a full belly. I could feel the hum of the emergency power source active under my feet as I walked around my room and when I got into bed I shut the door as always. In the darkness I lay awake, the soul person, real, awake and whole on the entire ship and I did feel apprehensive, as though this was not natural and yet totally real.

I thought of Ben and his touch, of Lucile and Gareth and even of Leon. How they were no longer with me. Remembrances of David and the scar on his left leg came to me, how he used to lay behind me and I could feel the scar tissue etching a pattern across his knee and rubbing against the back of my legs. How he would breathe deeply and that I would fall asleep while breathing in time with him. How comforting he had been in those first few months.

Lucile was always the one I would hug and I remembered her soft skin with its athletic frame underneath and most of all the scent of her, filling my head with thoughts of sex and gardens. She put something on her hair, a spray that smelt like my mother's roses. I would breathe in and let that aroma fill me up and close my eyes and at first I would love it. I would be able to see the roses and the garden and feel the sun on my face and skin and I'd smile. It was so evocative of the days before the painting that I would almost feel myself being moved to tears, something that I obviously controlled and contained. I was not one to weep in front of others.

Those nights with her would be filled with caresses, touching and long, exhausting orgasms but they would also bring dreams of my mother's garden and of peace disturbed by a noise coming from the bushes. I would look and see my mother and the gardener but also something else behind them, something in the bushes behind the roses. I would tell my mother to climb down off the gardener, to look out for there was something there, watching us, but she would ignore me and burry herself deeper into her act of union.

I would step past them, the sight of the gardener's buttocks being clawed at by mother's hands, her fingernails drawing blood. It would distract me every single time and I would spin to hear the bush burst open as an animal would come out low, take hold of my leg and drag me into the darkness. I would feel its breath on my face as I cowered against the brick wall and then look up to see the Black Panther bare its teeth at me. I would not cry out but wake and open my eyes still expecting to see that predator ready to devour me whole.

That was the reason I couldn't stay with her, I had had that dream many times before I'd ever met Lucile but she brought that animal with her every single night and it would prey on me, like I was its to kill whenever it wanted to and in truth I was. I was its victim and I only broke the cycle when I ended it with Lucile and remained on my own for some time afterwards. It wasn't that it terrified me or made me feel powerless, it was just something I couldn't understand and so something I had to be rid of.

That night I slept and could not smell Lucile's hair or feel her body pressing against mine in the darkness and yet I dreamed of the panther none the less.

CHAPTER ELEVEN

KING MINOS

In that first week a blur of activity pushed me through each day. I learned to respond to the alarm and fulfil my technical duties on board, checking the various gas levels and checking the energy buoy. It was easy and in fact took me no more than twenty minutes, included walking time from section to section. I walked past the grey walls into uniformed rooms full of technical equipment I knew little about and had less interest in. I did my duty and came to a slightly worrying conclusion; if my duties only took up a short period of time, minutes rather than hours, then I would have a lot of time to fill. At first this would be easy and wasn't really a problem but if I started to experience difficulties due to isolation then that short time would leave me inert for most of the day; useless and probably aware of the fact.

I ran three of my courses that week, I wasn't going to go crazy and hammer through the halls every day; I realised that I didn't actually enjoy the runs but I didn't want to become trapped in my living quarters either. I needed to make sure I didn't start seeing the ship as my enemy, we were in this together after all, and so I ran and forced myself to do a different course every two days.

As I ran through the sections and decks the ship didn't seem disrupted by the soft paddling of my impact absorbent footwear, instead I found the rhythmic beating brought a soul to the place, complete with a heartbeat. The faster my pace the more excited my companion became, and so she willed me on; The Buckingham and I, in collusion.

When not running I organised the two areas I would be using for my projects. Deck eight and deck fourteen may be close numerically but were actually in different sections, separated by a ten minute walk. I suppose this was designed to make sure I would have places to go other than the bridge, cryogenics, kitchen and bed, though I wouldn't tell you that was the only reason. It was probably something technical concerning the power relay and air filtration systems. Little did it matter really, what mattered was that I was given an area of over four thousand square feet on deck eight and the same on deck fourteen to do with what I liked. I could move the walls, change their colour, and reset environmental controls to effect minimal changes; there really was free reign for me there. I saw it as an opportunity to have two studios, two different places to pursue my art, the first; deck eight, a serious, colony driven scheme and the second; fourteen, would be my own personal space.

That first week I programmed the walls to change from their dull military grey to a far brighter white. I turned up the intensity of the light so that the walls practically glowed; like they were from a dream or perhaps a celestial waiting room. Both areas were clean, bright and ready and I filled them with paint pots and canvases. When the transportation of the equipment was done I selected the wall lay out from the pre existing suggestions on the computer and then watched them metamorphosis. I watched the space transform itself as the walls twisted around, driven by electrical impulses, like thoughts that fired complicated commands throughout the room, dancing around each other till they came to rest as a group of Ballroom Dancers would following the departure of the final notes of the orchestra.

I walked the long corridor on deck eight and selected rooms to be places to paint in and places to paint on; I was going to turn the place into an artwork all of its own. It was going to tell the story of the ships journey and of the people that lived and breathed on it for over three years before any of the colonists even took a step out onto their new world.

This story was not one of hardship or of toil but routine and discipline, co-operative efforts that led to the smooth running of the ship for over eighteen months. In those eighteen months nothing much had really happened of any note (at least not that I was aware of), everything had run like clockwork. Perhaps that's why Gareth and Lucile did what they did... No, I don't think it was boredom that brought them to that act, they were obviously attracted and I presume they had copulated previously to that incident so I must assume it was a way of intensifying their secret union, a way to covet excitement; an excitement that led to the transformation of five thousand and three people.

Thinking of how we had worked simply and sensibly for so long without incident brought me to a conclusion that I was not prepared for at that time; I had liked this journey. I had enjoyed it and the people that were busy with their own tasks and would look up to say 'thank you' but didn't really log me as a person to break their work to talk to until dinner time arrived. I had been less observed here than at any point in my life, left to entertain myself more than I'd ever dreamed possible and produced some works of art in the aft observation deck that I was particularly proud of. I even showed one to David as soon as I was sure it was done, something I rarely feel the need to do anymore; submit my work for approval.

This particular piece of work was an attempt to capture not just what a nebula looks like from the human eye but what it means to us, beyond the technical, past the purely ascetic, through the wonder and finally to land at the place where they all met and became an emotional reaction. I wanted this particular swirl of colours, though predominantly blue and red, to be something more than it was, perhaps something spiritual, and of course when you pursue meaning from the external and match it with the internal I believe you are searching for God. You are on a journey of the heart that can transform the whole.

A nebula is a vast cloud of dust and gas; Hydrogen, Helium and other ionized gases collect with the dust to form clumps that gather mass and so collect further material until they become stars, bright, blazing stars that gather material around them. This belt of gases around them forms into planets, moons and so Nebulas are the birthplaces of wonder, of light, of life.

David liked my view of the universe, the hard lines and sharp colours of the main structure indicating the rigidity of the physics; the inescapable truths that we have discovered. Soft blended swirls between spread off into the black, like thoughts and feelings, all of these things coming from the bright centre of forming stars, the God we know and the truth we have learnt melded together in one light; a light we cannot look upon directly as its emanation is too bright. The God in us reflected in the wonders around us. He stood staring at it for over five minutes before sitting down and taking my hands in his and telling me that he was jealous of my inner truth. I blushed and allowed his compliment to penetrate my outer peace and it gave me great joy.

I explained that the painting was covered in an imperceptible layer of translucent Graphene, designed to protect the image forever as it repelled any dust with a slight electrical charge. The picture could be touched, poked and interacted with but would not alter. More than this the Graphene screen was programmed to detect which colours it covered, on the back of the painting was an audio emitter that I'd programmed to emit the sound that the electromagnetic waves made if the frequency is dropped one point seven five trillion times, so making them audible. Combining a spectrographs findings, used to detect the electromagnetic waves, and the image I had been able to actually make the painting sing.

I activated the paintings emit mode and set it to play a recording I had made by moving my finger slowly around the painting, its volume adjusted to a level I found pleasant, and so the nebula sung to us. It's sound filling the dimly lit room, washing over us with its unearthly symphony of osculating cords and high pitched, throbbing, seemingly endless notes.

David was suitably impressed.

This was after we had split and he was nice to me even then, which I thought was logical but was not always how people interacted once a union came to its end. Sometimes there were harsh words and ill feelings, I had been on the giving and receiving end of both negative stances in my years and at the age of ninety eight I thought it was good that I had come through those childish plays to be sitting with a man who also knew the benefit of a properly controlled and reflective attitude towards deunification.

I wanted him to say that he loved it and he did, but without trying to rekindle our bond or seek sexual gratification as payment for his kind words. He looked at some of my other paintings and agreed that they needed work or that they were 'excellent' but this was the 'one.' The picture I had completed that proved that I was an artist that was well worth her place on a colonial ship that had struck out into the universe to bring prosperity and good to all humanity. We were to settle farther than anyone ever had and push our race even more into the realms of immortality, spreading our seed through the astral bodies like gods.

I slept well that night and completed my work with ease the next day. My first week alone on The Buckingham reminded me of how I felt the day after showing David 'The Nebula'; the discovery of something amazing that is shared, a plan is made and I, 'the artist,' set to producing something of great quality that would drive deeper into my soul and bring me closer to revealing God within.

With the spaces organised, my exercise routine worked out and embarked upon and the fail safes in place for systems monitoring I just had one thing left to start; I had to start to paint. Which area to start in? What to express first? How to go about it? All these questions came as very alien to me; I had always had a very organic way of working; I painted what I wanted to, when I wanted to. When the urge took me to capture something on canvas I would gather samples, feel the surfaces and touch the materials involved, play with the light and stare at my subject until it revealed its secrets. Some things would hold their secrets close and I would start painting them, putting washes on and bringing the basic structures to life and only then would it tell me its truths. Other objects would stand in the light and I would strip them bare with a glance and know what to capture of my subject, what was relevant and what was subterfuge attempting to the obscure the truth.

Here was a different problem and one that took me a week to crack. I sat on deck eight and placed easels and canvases and I knew I wanted to capture locations in the ship; objects and the people that had been there. I called up records of the men and women who designed and built the ship; the money men, the scientists and the diplomats, astronomers and chemists, leaders and followers. My father's face flashed onto the screen several times during my search, as he was an important part of the planning and financing of this new colony. I considered painting him but he struck me as a part of my individual past, too personal a figure to me for this project.

The crew all had faces to be painted, the custodial crew, the council leaders, the security executives, the children. I would place their faces on the walls of the gallery, looking into the room. I would find a way to represent the people undertaking this incredible journey, show the humanity and the hope of the species as we pushed out into the universe, making it a smaller and smaller place with every step. I was excited to come to an understanding with the space I was going to transform and gratified that it was so easy to see the transformation that I would make inside it.

Sitting on deck fourteen was a more frustrating experience. I would sit and play with the lighting and the colour of the walls, marvelling at the versatility of the Graphene in the plastic walls conducting the electricity and wondering if we really did understand how incredible was our story, from evolving into ape, to man, to dominant species, warrior, lover, soldier, criminal, lawyer, Hunter, holy man, scientist, mother, father, doctor, victim, peacekeeper, terrorist, student, colonist, artist and everything in between. We pushed out to places that our ancestors simply watched, thinking those bright dots in the night sky were gods, and not knowing God was within them all.

I sat in that space and changed its colour and shape and at the end of each session I reset it to how I had found it; a long corridor leading down to a small end room, the corridor had doors springing off into rooms every seven feet. As soon as you walked in your eye was drawn to the final room, but what was to be held there that commanded such focus from me when I entered the deck?

By the end of the week the work on deck eight was taking shape in my head, I had the structure of the main piece in place and had worked out how to do it. Obviously I knew I was going to be on this ship for at least seven months; that was Ben's prediction, but I knew these situations didn't pan out as anyone planned them to and I had the potentially unpleasant reality that I could be alone for far longer. In that time I wanted to have the bulk of the work done and so would use everything that was at my disposal to complete the walls and the displays as well. I envisioned myself in deck eight for most of the week, preparing and working, painting and modifying and if I had the need for a personal project I would conduct the business on deck fourteen. That's how it was going to work.

In the second week I selected a different wall setting for deck eight, I created a large hall like space in the centre with a corridor that ran around it on the outside. The corridor had several rooms off it to be used as storage and I made a workshop near the entrance for materials and stored a workbench to build displays. Deck fourteen remained white and singular in its mission to draw you toward that final room. I couldn't escape the feeling that whatever was to occur there was not something I was ready for yet and so left it as it was. It perplexed me that I could be so blank about one place and yet so full of inspiration for another. I wondered what that said about me. I wasn't worried or even concerned, just conscious of the emptiness that was my personal space.

I walked to deck eight and its clear challenge with a light step, ate well and always made sure I was where I was meant to be in those weeks. It seemed important to be doing and I thrust myself into the task like a duellist would pierce the flesh of his opponent to ensure his continued existence and in many ways that was true to the situation. I did not want to be become a mythical king presiding over a maze that no living thing walked in, only to be found wandering the halls some years later, deranged and babbling, or perhaps hang myself from the top of a tall staircase; my last friend being the rope that ended my suffering. I needed the ship to be a partner in this time, it and I, The Buckingham and Gita against the universe.

I would not become terrified of the empty corridors as I would fill them with my footfalls as I ran and the promise of artistic glory with my paint and vision. I was not trapped, I was free.

CHAPTER TWELVE

WALLS HAVE SMILES

Nearly five hundred thousand souls on the ship and yet I had embarked on bringing as many of them to life as possible, so obviously I needed to represent them all in some way without painting each one individually. I started by making sure I had all the 'important' people logged in my files, then I asked the computer to select whole families, then select one representative from each one randomly. From there I asked for racial filters to bring in the correct proportion of colours that made up the colony, then sex, then hair colours, and from that honed down list I wanted the computer to feed all their faces through the files so I could see them.

I looked through the files and had those faces implanted onto the wall in front of me. A new face would flash up every six seconds and I would sit on my bean bag, brought up from the survival container, and chew on vegetable snacks while saying yes or no. In two weeks I had gone through the slide show three times and was the happy owner of a list of faces only two thousand strong. From those numbers I selected my favourite two hundred people. To make the list the subject needed to stand out, they needed to have character, personality, exceptional beauty or an alternative look; something that removed them from the pack.

I viewed those faces and had to admit that we were a near perfect looking race at present. All of us bar the very rare (like David) seemed to be forever young, athletic, disease free individuals with good teeth and well looked after hair. We dressed in various colours and styles and our dedication to keeping our self image at near or on peak fitness made us not just physically attractive but it also tied us together. We were a race that evolved together and had gone out of our way to remove the differences that had driven our peoples apart in the past. The only thing we really left alone was the colour of our skins but then the races had interbred so much in the thousands of years we had co-existed that someone of 'pure' colour was quite rare now.

Of course people still carried racial genes but they were normally mixed so even if the colour of the person next to you was different you would always have a physical similarity in the eyes, nose, skull or jaw. We were a blended race of explorers who had outgrown our childish hatreds, or maybe instead of outgrowing them we had more accurately fought until those differences no longer mattered and that the commonalities of our lives outweighed the differences.

When did we become this 'one being', or at least form this greater bond? Did it happen in one apocalyptic night when fire burst down from the sky? No. It was a slow and hard process of breaking the bonds of oppression and hatred that took thousands of years to build. We had tribal, family, national, continental, world, civil and religious wars till finally we woke in a society that loved more than it hated.

For thousands of years the religious war and disagreement forged an axis of power with paranoia and politics and drove the people of Homeworld to kill for land, title and love of a common God. Then came world conflicts and advancements in technology that spelled the end of our race as a structured and dominant being and so we calmed. We looked and we spoke and those feelings of mistrust still filled our leader's hearts and heads with hate and distrust but they knew the conclusion to war with missiles and energies that could not be contained, so we spoke more.

It calmed and warmed and calmed and warmed for a long time before Doctor Felix Armitage and his aides developed the drug dubbed 'The Immortality Pill.' When it was first trialled there was an equal reaction of happiness and horror, now we could live forever as the pill would bolster our immune system and maintain our physical form from the day we took it. Aging and most diseases ended and many predicted that the world would perish now, not because of war but starvation; there would be too many of us to feed, clothe and employ.

Felix Armitage took many years to make his transformation from man to messenger, or perhaps the people simply took many years to truly listen to what he was saying? Probably the later. Yet when he brought out his book, just fifty pages long, able to be transported to any electrical device for free, paid for by him and so free to the people of Homeworld; it was met with outrage. How dare he take the three holy books and tamper with them? How dare he remove the rules that governed religious societies and formed the structure of faith? He had to be stopped!

It was as though they had forgotten that they had spent the last two thousand years and more dictating an ever changing text to the masses that favoured guilt over freedom, blame over self governance, hate over love and rules over compassion.

That time would stereotypically be depicted as a terrified world, tearing itself to pieces and burning the innocent along the way and yet that is not how it happened. There were those that rose up and demonstrated and issued Armitage with death threats, especially when he tongue in cheek referred to himself as 'Jesubrahmed', and yet he acted the part. He kept nominal amounts of money to himself and gave all he had to charity, preached peace where there was hatred and implored the world to seek solutions based on science and long term coping strategies rather than warring over natural resources like Oil and water.

It took one hundred years or so of arguing and fighting, of reform and diplomacy before most of the world agreed that whether you loved, believed, ignored or even hated him made little difference, he had a point. With more and more converting to 'unificationalism' or 'trinity thought', the combination of Judaism, Christianity and Islam (with an attitude of total acceptance towards other faiths) took the fire from the world and brought a form of platform that the scientists could use to bring solutions.

Humanity needed to tackle the population quandary and had developed all the technology in that time to do so while the politicians and priests threw words the scientists fired probes and missions into the heavens, discovered new elements and defeated problems that kept us planet locked. They build alternative energy cells and particle accelerators to lay the universe bare for us to see all its secrets and even then we learned only enough to allow us to know that we needed to know more.

As the social structure transformed leaving the carcass of mass poverty and singular state economics in its wake the spiritual and scientific met to ask the most important question we had ever asked; where was our future to lie? The answer came in the stars and we, as a race, pushed to find the answers, knowing that the growing population would become ever more impossible to manage.

'Jesubrahmed', as he was now known, brought the 'Expansion of The Race ' to the world when he appealed to the people to ease a burden by reaching within themselves and asking if they were ready to take the step needed to colonise other worlds. Billions agreed and so the task was launched. We mined asteroid fields and created giant ships, took the engines that could breach the speed of light and packed those ships with people. We set out to continue our evolution by populating far off worlds that the scientists had already confirmed were life sustaining planets. Those first ships cast themselves into the universe knowing it would take hundreds of years to reach their destinations, packed full of people in cryogenic pods that put their faith in the wisdom of Jesubrahmed, but more importantly in the skill and strength of their scientists and leaders.

It astounds me still to think that they went without the planning that we do now and yet against all odds succeeded so many times. Colonies in systems far and wide now thrive and grow and there is evidence that evolution is taking a course of its own and making us even better at adapting and changing.

Out of the Billions of people that set out into the universe very few have been lost in large numbers. Of course there is the 'Indo star', the subcontinent colony ship that is still lost, said to be host to fifty million people, the 'Rio' that exploded when struck by a rogue meteorite killing the thirty million people on board instantly and of course The Osprey, but apart from those instances the colonial ships survived against the odds.

Now we ourselves were against the odds, alone, surrounded by the ever expanding universe, our lives held within a huge colonial ship made insignificant in size by the space around us.

I looked at faces I selected and knew this would be a piece of work that would consume my thoughts. I knew it was what I needed and so swallowed my concern at entering such a vast project and dived in with both feet leaving deck fourteen white, clear, bright and filled with the absence of my artistic input.

Two-hundred portraits? It was a huge task to undertake and I realised I would need to make as much use of the technology surrounding me as I could. I programmed the walls to a standard off-white colour and altered the texture of the surface so that it was rough, as though the walls had been evenly scratched all over. I used this texture so that it would take paint straight onto the surface and then placed sheets of rolled plasti-monitor over most of the surfaces from floor to ceiling. Each sheet showed roughly the same image; perfectly sculpted bodies, both male and female in grey, skin tight jumpsuits; the very suits my fellow colonists wore in their cryogenic sleep. The front rank was filled with the colonists and crew that were important or of interest; namely those that had made the final two thousand but not the final two hundred. They were standing at the front of vast crowds, all made up of the colonists, the computer projecting their faces onto these standardised bodies. They were all looking in, all still, inanimate, alive and yet imposed by the computer core and so without any soul.

Every five feet there was a blank person at the front, an image omitted leaving a strange absence of character in the panel; character I would fill with a hand rendered image of their form. There were two hundred of these gaps on the walls and I intended to fill each one with one of my chosen colonists, few would be subjected to my artistic eye out of the mass and yet the mass were also represented. It felt right to be looking at them projected onto the wall and when I started painting my first subject I had an incredible rush of excitement and joy, as though I understood that this was something that would bring me interest and peace and would be looked back at with some amazement (at least I hoped it would).

I had considered lining the walls with the faces of those that had lost their lives in the accident and instantly knew that was the wrong thing to do. The colonists of this new world would first have to come to terms with was not just the rigorous set up of an entire infrastructure but of the grief felt for the transformations of five thousand people, they did not need to have to face a permanent record of all the lost souls straight away. That tribute could wait until the colony was properly established. No, this was to be a positive piece, designed to show our unity and bond in the undertaking of a colossal adventure.

I worked to set up the main room first and checked how it would look by walking around the corridors and rooms repeatedly, those faces staring out at me. I didn't find them scary or judgemental, they were with me, supporting me and in some small part I thought of them as the spirit of the ship itself; of the engine core and mainframe that would be used on the planet when they finally arrived. I watched these people looking at me and knew I would miss them when I left the room and sure enough when I walked home for dinner I felt lonely.

The walk back to my quarters and dinner that night made me think of what I needed to do next, on deck eight I had created a heavily populated area and one that was meant to be a piece of art, what if I decided to do the same in other areas? It took me just twenty feet of corridor walking to know what I would do next, what the next logical step for me was. I would create dinner guests to share my meal with each night. I had chairs and small canvases so what was to stop me from looking up and seeing a face I knew? Nothing!

I prepared my dinner of rice and curry that night and ate heartily, knowing company would be coming soon to that room. I washed up and then headed to my quarters to change and prepare for bed and there I sat, on the end of my bed, having pulled my boots off but not persisted any further, thinking of who I was going to invite to the table. I knew this would grow and be fun and also be equally uncomfortable some days but I was as set upon it as I was the project on deck eight.

I showered and cleansed and used the laser shaver to maintain the same look I had had for the last seventy years, a complete lack of body hair bar my eyebrows and head of hair. This soft, sleek frame of mine slipped between the sheets and I felt something I had not for two weeks; I was aroused.

Was it because I had thought of those eyes watching me while in the shower? Was constructing Ben's face in my head and how I would paint it onto my canvas as the water rolled down my skin what produced this reaction? I didn't know, I just knew I was in need of sexual gratification. I was a person with a strong and powerful imagination and so I conjured Ben's body in my mind, the thought of his touch, the depth he reached inside me and the taste of his kisses. It took me no time at all to reach climax and after twenty minutes I was ready and willing to repeat the exercise, this time taking far longer, allowing my imagination to wander through other scenarios and gathering Ben till he was more of a man than perhaps he had been; I made him more forceful, energetic and probing. My eyes squeezed tightly as I again climaxed and this time lay back feeling calm and fulfilled. I switched out the light and slept deeply till the alarm woke me the next day.

CHAPTER THIRTEEN

A QUESTION UNANSWERED

Four weeks in and deck eight was taking shape; bursting into colour in fact. I checked the files on my subjects and selected images that showed them on Homeworld. They wore clothes that differed from the grey jump suits, some showing more flesh and others more style. Different weaves and materials was a theme I found myself working in, bringing these people to life and showing their individuality as part of the collective and, of course, following one of Jesubrahmed's points; that being an individual does not break you from the collective, it doesn't separate you from God, in fact it is that spark of individuality which indicates where God sits in all of us.

The first few figures were rough sketches on the walls, swipes of colour and base forms, in different poses to the thousands around them and yet they stood with the collective. I would eat lunch looking at these mad eccentrics in this sea of grey and I loved their personality and their presence. They made me feel like I was part of this mission, part of the colony and reminded me that I was still surrounded by people, of all types, glued together by the common need to grow and create communities wherever they went. These brave individuals that had decided to build their community in space.

My runs took me further a field and I found myself learning to appreciate the twists and turns of the ships corridors like never before. I stopped and checked on individual cryogenic pods to watch them sleep and sometimes even saw one of my subjects in their torpor, unaware of my sober face studying them for deeper meaning.

In truth I was happiest when busy and could drive myself to incredible ends when I wanted too, so in the evenings I had taken to sleeping less and painting the portraits that would eventually sit on the chairs I would position around my table to eat. Meals I ate with one hand while the other was used to sketch something I had seen of interest that day, perhaps a comic strip of my actions so far, the glass that contained the water I drank, fragments of art and perception that spilled from me all of the time.

Post dinner I would make sure I was observing the basic survival skills that were suggested to keep me or any other stranded crew member sane. I watched small amounts of documentaries, engaged in a physical activity like yoga or Pilates and masturbated, perhaps not every night but certainly I tried to bring my sex drive to a normal level and maintain it with toys and fantasy. I also brought one of my sleeping partners into the bed every couple of days. I programmed them with the weight I thought would bring the most level of normalcy to my sleep and then cuddled them. At first I found it strange and almost depressing but it became more normal with each passing night and soon I looked forward to climbing into bed with the warm, inanimate, rough form of Ben and enjoyed reading to him or Victoria, depending whose turn it was. It didn't take me long to brake my vow not to name the dummies; I enjoyed them far more once I'd actually named them.

Victoria hadn't been the first women I was engaged in union with but she was the one I cared most about. When we broke our bond it took all my effort not to resort to childish and rude behaviour and even then I feel I failed in that respect. She is the person I believe hurt me the most in this sort of relationship, even so I wanted her now.

I programmed the female sleep aid to be fuller of bust and slightly wider of hip, then increased it in weight and clothed it. The result was a poor replacement for her supple, muscular body but when all I was going to get from her was sleep that didn't seem to matter. It was a mental exercise but one that I was urged to remember was just that and I was not to immerse myself too deeply within my fantasy; something I was good at sticking to for the most part.

I was lying in bed, reading a book out loud to my sleeping partner when the text made me laugh. I wasn't a natural laugher, if I'm honest I have to confess I didn't even smile that often, but this was a paragraph that took me by surprise and brought that almost alien noise out of me. I buried my head against Victoria's handcrafted shoulder and as I raised my head again and regained control I kissed the sleeping aids shoulder. It was a peck, yet I looked at the dummy and realised that it had been a show of affection for this adjustable bundle of cloth and simulated breaths.

There was silence and I felt conscious of my solitude for a minute before I regained control and placed the book down gently on my bedside table and switched off the light. I rolled over and hugged it tight but as I would a pillow, not a lover. I squeezed it tight and switched off the breathing and heat production device in the sleeping aid, turning it into a very expensive, very large cushion.

In the morning I woke from fitful dreams with my right hand resting on her t-shirt covered breast and decided that a few nights alone would have to follow that uncomfortable night with my long gone lover. Victoria was the second woman to break my heart, the first, of course, had been my mother.

*

My mother was a woman who loved life and I loved her for that. It's true that much of what I say about her is negative or perhaps overly cutting but it doesn't mean I hate her or that she killed the love we had, not at all, it's just who she was and who I became weren't compatible.

Her name was Helena and she was a beautiful woman when she met my father and still is today. Of course we all look very athletic now in the most part and care greatly for our appearance but she was a woman who drew glances from all with her perfectly turned out visage and her stunning looks, her soft, pale skin made her look fragile and her flame red hair brought a warning of passion. I am not very much like her physically; I'm slightly shorter than the average at 5ft 6ins, though I have a long body and legs so I look taller than perhaps I first appear, while she is tall and statuesque. My breasts are small and firm and I have a toned and athletic frame as most others do around me, she is voluptuous and is in her own words 'built and driven to love and lust.' I don't stand out like she does and when we stand next to each other it is often said we 'couldn't be more different.'

I have dark skin; my father's family were originally from Sri-Lanka, before it became part of the Asian principality of course, and I have high cheek bones and short, dark hair that I keep in a bob. My eyes are dark and I have a wider nose than my predominantly Caucasian mother. I've never been told that my eyes are 'deep and consuming' or that my looks 'floor men' like she did and yet it really doesn't bother me. I keep my looks functional and rarely apply make-up as I generally don't feel the need to impress people with my outer image; this is just a shell after all, a well maintained shell but a shell none the less.

She was not the first woman the king of the Union Of Briton copulated with but she was the one that he decided he would marry and with her consent they became paired for life; a rare thing to do at this time as 'life' can theoretically mean forever. The oldest human alive that I know of is over three hundred years old and he of course is 'Jesubrahmed,' so to pledge to live together 'forever' is a very large commitment to make and yet one they made willingly. She accepted and joined the old institution that had lost nearly all of its glamour and power but none of its allure. King and queen? She was in heaven; at least she was for the first few years.

Sadly they were not a very sensible pairing in my view and as it turns out they agree as they now spend very little time together and enjoy a very open marriage, though enjoy is probably the wrong word to use. Suffice to say that they were very much in love when they first unified and for many years stayed that way. He had taken the small amount of money given to him by the state for carrying on the royal line and invested it in colonial exploits and amassed a large fortune, she loved to spend his money and make rash decisions while he would consider everything. He would procrastinate while she leapt in head first and inevitably she was considered a very exciting person to be around because of her reckless attitude while he seemed greyer than before.

As those first years passed she became famous in her own right for her passion and lack of control, but also for her compassion. She would give his money away as much as she could to help people less fortunate than them, for though mass starvation and poverty were a thing of the past really still there are always varying degrees of wealth. He meanwhile, shipped millions of people off to new worlds, giving them futures that they could forge themselves.

In this vein they continued, though now they worked separately, he building wealth through business and organising colonial expeditions, making sure that the people would be looked after while she focused on the Homeworlders, gathered her own fortune through product endorsement, public speaking and modelling. She coveted fame and the Homeworlders loved her for it. In time they were different people and she used his company and name to build her reputation while he used her to raise funds and gather press for new endeavours and expeditions. Neither of them were bad people, they were just different. When they had me many were shocked as it was seen as obvious to the outside world that they were about to split, but they were as stubborn as they were attractive and brilliant and so stayed together.

I was the product of an attempt to bring them closer together and that worked for six years until I unveiled the painting and then they reverted to old ways only with more zest. My father was convinced that burying himself in work and the maid would help the situation (I'm not sure what the maid thought but I can imagine she got paid extra for the overtime). My mother saw no reason to be discrete anymore and so threw herself into a lifestyle of public engagements and private liaisons.

The weird thing really was that they would still copulate and sleep in the same bed. It was as though they just ignored all the things they did outside of the home or when they weren't together; that it didn't matter as long as they stayed together. It's still how they live now and when I used to catch them laughing together or watching vid on the sofa I'd want to ask them how they can be who they were? Act how they were acting, and yet still be together? Perhaps the truth is that they are far more grown up than I am, that they know what they want and that is to be together, it's just that they also understand that they alone are not enough for each other and so have come to accept that others will always be waiting in the wings.

I don't understand and I don't think I need to, they are who they are and I am who I am; a product of their union that acts nothing like them. I don't want to be like them, have never felt the need to copy them and don't see the merit in the choices they make, but then the feeling I think is mutual.

I worked as they wished me to for many years after I had started to paint, but as soon as choice became a factor I ceased all technical courses and education and immersed myself in art. I went to seminars, took long journeys exploring Homeworld and its natural wonders and lived off my allowance (which was sizable then and still is now). My father was livid with me and stopped my payments many times but when I did not call and beg him to give me money he started crediting my account again. My mother sometimes came to see me in those days of high adventure but we were not alike for the most part, I wasn't in Italy to drink and copulate, I was there to capture its spirit. So she crawled all over the waiters and singers and I looked on in disgust.

She stayed until I stopped dinning with her and the local man she had decided to copulate with and so she would go home and tell my father that I was not serious about my art and that I was on a permanent holiday. This would upset me but I understood her reaction, I had always looked down on her for being weak when it came to copulation and she had reacted with her own dismissive attitude when it came to my love for painting. She would argue that an image can be captured digitally that was exact in every detail and so would be better than any painting, I argued that a painting can tell people more than just what happened but why, how and more importantly how it made people feel. The artist could show others the emotion of all involved. She would dismiss this as ego, I would call her shallow, she would indicate I was frigid, I would say I had taste and did not copulate with just anyone, for me there needed to be some interest other than that of my loins. This would bring the silence and an inevitable plane ticket home for her.

How, when we were aware of each other's distain for the other did she break my heart? How did she penetrate the thick armour I had built up around it? It was a simple thing. She was asked in public once how she viewed my art and replied 'I try not to.' Perhaps she was having a bad day, perhaps she was trying to be funny, more likely she was simply not really bothered with the fall out that her comment would bring. It was the weekend of my first public exhibition and I faced the press with the hope of pledging myself to this endeavour for years to come and ended up answering questions about my rift with my mother and why she was my strongest critic.

I have too much pride to cry normally but at the end of that first night I waited for everyone to leave and then sat amongst my work and wept. It was only for a short time and I know I can't have them back but I resented every single tear that fell. I was angry more at myself than at her really. I had invited her to come and open the exhibition with me but she told me she was already booked. It turns out she was booked into a table at the Ritz with Croon Tumar, world famous master of hypnosis. She didn't go home that night and neither did I.

The exhibition was a great success and many hailed it as the start of a new and important artistic journey; 'one that will sweep those fortunate enough to see Askari's work into an intoxicating world of wonder and truth.' My mother and I have never spoken of that night and I presume we never will.

CHAPTER FOURTEEN

A PARTY OF FIVE

I wanted to know how many people I wanted at my dinner table and so on that first night it seemed wise to invite them all. The portraits sat on chairs and stared at me as I ate; observing the table manners my father was so keen for me to learn at a young age.

All seven paintings were rough and still needed work but were good enough to bring here so they could view each other. As I looked up I was struck by how strange I thought my selections had turned out to be. Why these seven faces from my past had come here was beyond me, I had been struck by the urge to paint them and so had. In the five weeks I had been doing them in the evenings after the deck eight marathons I had been forced to allow my hands to work instinctively and this was the result? I finished my soup and wiped my lips with a napkin and saw my father staring at me, no sign of a slight smile just that blank expression they all had. I picked up my bread and wiped it round the bowl to see if I could get a reaction, he didn't move, so I bolted my drink down in one and wiped my mouth with the back of my sleeve; nothing. I shook my head and smiled, perhaps this was going to be more fun than I had first thought?

My father was sitting to my right; his portrait a full face view; the rest of him was in a meeting (I smiled to myself). Mother was next to me on my left, full face view again; the rest of her was busy under the gardener (I didn't smile, I judged). Lucile I had painted in profile as I had last seen her, her face caught in that moment of ecstasy, her skin pale and her eyes squeezed tightly closed; the rest of her was stuck to Gareth (less amusing still but I couldn't stop this game now I had started it).

I poured myself some more water and looked down as I sipped my drink. I looked up at the other portraits, impossibly I was becoming very self conscious of my honesty towards them and tried to defeat that feeling by saying what I thought out loud; to ram home the fact they couldn't hear me.

'Ivan, the rest of you is stuck under a machine,' it wasn't that hard after all (and I knew he couldn't stare at me as he was deep in space, fast asleep, yet still those eyes did indeed stare directly out at me). 'David; stuck in my past,' I felt mean as I looked at his full face portrait and realised I'd painted him slightly too grey (Why was I placing a man I respected into something as narrow and dismissive as past tense?).

Two canvases sat at the end of the table next to each other, both of men and though one was very influential in my life the other was not, so why had I painted him? If he meant nothing to me of lasting importance then why was he here? I watched them for a reaction and knew the game had come too far already, but it was one I had to finish.

'Ben, my Future?' I looked at the face and couldn't understand how or why I had started this stupid game (my eyes traced his face, the lines and the depth of colour and I realised I had spent more time on his portrait than all the others). Finally the man that I leant nothing and yet everything from sat waiting to be classified. I had painted him looking to the left in profile, not looking at me as he had spent most of his time doing; after all it was beneath him to address me directly most of the time.

'Salvador Iranie,' I said aloud and watched for that mouth to twitch. It didn't. 'A coward.' He took it like I knew he would; how he should have, and I expected to feel the pressure release from my shoulders but it didn't. I hadn't thought of him in so long, blocked his face from my normal thoughts. It struck me I had made a grave error in selecting him for my table. Why would this abusive man sit with me at all? Why would I want him to? Maybe that's why I had done it; capturing him and forcing him to watch me eat as he so hated doing in life, punishing him for his cruelty.

The meal was finished and I decided I was not in the mood for pudding so left and washed up. The kitchen was full of highly technical equipment designed to make work in the kitchen both easier and more efficient and yet I avoided using it. I had always found washing up and other manual tasks relaxing, ideas formed and grew while my hands were busy and so I washed up in the sink, peeled the vegetables with my own hands and cooked whenever I could. I don't know who decided there was no joy to be found in the preparation of food but whoever it was clearly missed the joy of creating and providing for yourself and your fellow diners. I walked back into the dining room and they were still sitting there, waiting.

I switched the light off and watched the canvases sit motionless in the dark. What would they say about me once I had left? Could these seven people have anything in common at all? Unlikely. No, they would sit in silence and whenever anyone tried to bring in a topic for discussion Salvador would burn them with his acidic words and make them feel worthless.

I left the paintings in the room and walked ten feet down the corridor before turning on my heels and re-entering the room. I picked up Salvador, Ivan and Lucile and placed them in the storage cupboard, then I pulled their chairs back so that breakfast could be enjoyed by the five of us; Father, Mother, David, Ben and of course myself. I got as far as the door again before I retrieved Lucile from that cupboard and placed her in the kitchen so she did not have to stay with the two hurtful men that would inevitably ignore each other all night.

Leaving the room for a final time I arrived at my quarters quickly, undressed, showered and changed for bed. Obviously I was overtired as I found myself fidgeting as I sat on the end of the bed, feeling exposed. I walked across the room and retrieved the male sleeping companion from the chair he sat on during the day and pulled him into bed with me. There I lay, attempting to sleep with the light on. I had never been able to do that and so after twenty minutes or so I forced myself to turn out the light and snuggled close to the pillow. After another hour I gave in and switched the breathing mode on and drifted to sleep spooning with me cushioned partner.

That night the Panther returned and when her breath was on my face she drew down even closer; I felt her teeth scratch across my cheeks. I woke up in the middle of the night and read for the remainder of my time in bed.

Sleep would not be an easy thing to find in the months to come and it was almost certainly this night that brought that terrible drought of rest upon me.

In the morning I knew I would have to do something to wrestle control back from my emotions. Having read Jesubrahmed's handbook in the small hours of the morning I decided an early breakfast and a punishing run would start my efforts to regain control, then I would gather the supplies I needed and head to deck eight. That day I had to listen to the alarms to lead me around and did my duty checking the statuses when I found myself walking past the mortuary, as I did every day. I stepped in when normally I would walk past and looked at the stasis chamber where Lucile, Gareth and Leon were stored. I don't know why I did it that day but I did and of course they were all as they had been left, frozen in time until a proper analysis of their bodies could be done by the investigators. I had captured Lucile's facial expression almost perfectly in my portrait and was impressed by just how much like her it was, though perhaps she was more beautiful than I had depicted her the position and arch of her neck was almost identically replicated. I wondered what she was thinking when she died and whether she knew she would be transformed in that last split second.

Standing there, watching their bodies intertwined it was hard not to look at Lucile and Gareth, propped against the wall and as my eyes were drawn to them; I was still in awe at the story their bodies told, a story of passion and fulfilment, of lust and exultation. It was in direct opposition to the body of Leon who lay in the corner on his back, blue and rigid and lifeless. This vision stood before me and it struck me that I had seen it before, this was something I knew.

It took me a few short seconds to realise that they were in the same basic positions as my first real success; the painting that my father and mother had sat up and discussed once I was in bed. It was as though the roses had been brought to life. I stepped back and turned away from them to make sure I had perspective, to be certain that I was not seeing more than was actually there. When I looked back they were still replicating my depiction of the roses.

I was unsure how to react. How would a normal person react? Should I be upset by what I saw or could I just walk away and smirk at the likeness their transformations had placed them in? Or was the universe playing a trick on me? Was I was being taunted by this vision at a time when I was understandably more vulnerable than normal?

I took a final look and decided they should stay where they were and realised I was already late for my jobs. I left, walking quickly and with a determined edge, I would take these possibly disturbing, perplexing days and I would push them aside. I would throw myself into my work on deck eight and when the alarm went for dinner I would face my decisions with a clear head. I would be tired but I always felt better after I had painted and so I would be in a far better frame of mind to deal with the problems now assaulting me, problems almost certainly brought on by my isolation.

The day progressed well and though fatigue was a factor in my diminished productivity and vision I still managed to step back at the end of the day and be pleased with my efforts. I looked around at the thousands and thousands of faces looking at me passively. I watched them staring out and smiled as I had started to recognise some of them and knew where they were cryogenically frozen. One woman drew my eye particularly; a woman I found attractive far beyond the others.

Around the corner there was a man that delivered a similar impact. I smiled at her and wondered how she moved and whether she would find me attractive on the colony? Could she be a possible future partner?

I had an artistic interest in the singular people of my project but she was one I thought of while running and I looked for her whenever I entered the deck. She had a slightly rounded face and an oriental completion, almond eyes and jet black long hair. Her face stood out and I could tell you it was because of the symmetry of its make up or its high cheek bones and slim covering and slightly fuller than normal lips for her racial base but in truth it was something else; something deeper.

I walked away thinking of her that night and that thought followed me all the way to the kitchens. I walked in and selected from my pre prepared menu and cooked quickly using the microwave. I said hello to Lucile as she watched me walk out of the door and into the dining area where my other eating companions waited for me.

I sat down and cast my eyes out to look at my guests, the steam rising off my noodles and beef strips, complimented perfectly with slightly crunchy vegetables and glass of water. I nodded and smiled at them feeling tired but far more in control than the night before.

'Good evening,' I said civilly to the collected canvases and started to consume my meal. I enjoyed every mouthful and even congratulated myself on cooking so well, serving up the perfect thing for the evening. I washed the food down and then went back for desert which I returned with; apple pie and custard.

'I saw a woman today, she didn't see me of course, but she was beautiful and I can't decide whether I would want to copulate with her or simply paint her over and over again. It's a line I suppose that many of you wouldn't understand but there is such a line in my head and I'm confused as to how I feel.' I looked up from my apple pie and felt quite natural discussing this with them, as though they were here to listen to me as opposed to the normal social diagram which placed me as the natural listener.

'I would tell you what she looks like but it would be pointless, what I want to know is how this makes you feel?' Was I playing with fire; talking to myself? David had told me to do what comes naturally when feeling lonely or depressed and though I was neither of those things I presumed that this was a time when normal people would feel such emotions and so decided to play it out.

'Father, I know you would be thrilled if this was a partnership that led to a long term union, while mother here would want me to let my hair down and follow my instincts and animal passions and pursue this woman until I had fulfilled all my desires,' I gave her a look and she did not confirm or deny my suppositions, instead she looked at my father, sitting opposite her, with an impassive, yet slightly amused smile. I looked back to check and indeed I had imagined the smile. She was as straight faced as she had been the night before.

'David, I think you would issue caution and suggest that I paint her first, gather my thoughts and emotions and make sure my motives are good before entering into any relationship with her be it professional or personally driven.' I cocked an eyebrow as David sometimes did when giving advice but I was sure he took this as some out of character fun on my part and so retained his relaxed manor and easy charm.

'Ben,' I paused as I had another mouthful, starting to enjoy myself when normally I would find speaking with so many people off putting. 'I think you'd be worried that she was going to steel me away from you but on seeing her you would almost certainly be very interested in seeing if she liked both of us enough to accept an invitation to enjoy us as a couple.' I smiled at him and knew in my head that he would pull a face and question whether he would ever share me with someone else in any circumstance.

'I think I would paint her several times and if I found her as attractive still I would see if she would join me, and perhaps I would ask her if Ben could come to.' The last of my dessert was finished and my refilled glass of water empty so I sat back and breathed out feeling a hundred times better.

'Now that's out of the way I have to tell you that we are going to follow some basic rules at these dinners,' I spoke loudly enough that the men in the cupboard would hear and I had left the door open to the kitchen so I could see Lucile easily from where I sat. 'We will have no more than five at the table including myself and I reserve the right to dine alone when I feel the need. Also we must all come to understand that we will rotate the guests so that you will all get to sit here and congregate but if I find you upsetting then I will remove you from the room and you will stay in the cupboard. Is that understood?' Silence followed so at least we didn't have a mutiny on our hands yet.

'Now we will not always discuss things that are pleasant or happy, sometimes we will argue and I'm sure sometimes I will upset you, just know that you are my canvases and if you become disruptive or too much trouble then I will black wash you and push you out of an airlock. Understood?' Again silence greeted my statements and that was almost certainly a signal that all had understood the situation and that they were in agreement.

'Finally, this does not mean that I'm cracking up or think that you are in any way alive, you are canvases and here to help me through what may prove to be a difficult time, so please do not misjudge uncharacteristic openness for insanity. That would be a grave error on your part.' My guests were obviously in full understand and agreement.

    I washed up and left the room, this time with a far more optimistic outlook on my dinner companions. Could this actually be a good idea that would see me able to talk through any problems that I have? I would have to wait and see.

I prepared for bed and slipped between the sheets with my female sleeping partner and masturbated while thinking of her body pressing against mine. Later I dragged Ben back into bed and we would all be there together. I had a massive orgasm, perhaps the biggest I had ever felt and slept deeply till the alarm. The panther was gone for now and I would continue to keep him at bay for as long as I could but of course I knew he would come back for me at some point.

CHAPTER FIFTEEN

STATUES

In the months that followed I would have dinner with my companions four times a week and breakfast would be shared with one or two only. Sometimes I would have Ivan or Salvador out so they could sit and watch me eat. I would drink my coffee and watch Ivan as he sat doing nothing and try to work out if my estimation of him was right or if I'd been harsh, and if so then was that what put him off the night he shared with Sheena? Could our discussion at dinner have made him a poor lover for the night or was he always 'coming up short'? I didn't know and inevitably I would be none the wiser when my cup was empty.

The work on deck eight wasn't all consuming and I slowed my pace to allow more time to paint the ship and its activities. I captured the kitchen and the bridge, observation deck and some of the cryogenic compartments. Two places eluded my eye though, the dining room and the room where Lucile, Gareth and Leon were transformed. No matter what I did, what time I came to those places and set up my easel, how much light I poured into the rooms or how much I thought about them before I started I simply could not capture what it was about them that was special. Those places had been transformed and what was unique about them had nothing to do with how they looked, it was now about how they 'felt' that was important. I needed to find another 'way in' but they always dodged my eye for detail and my imagination would not conjure the code to lay their secrets bare. They were enigmas that forced me to retreat, the bitter taste of defeat in my mouth.

I came to the conclusion that to unlock the mystery I would have to explore my feelings towards those places, towards those people. But how to start?

It was with some trepidation that I set up my easel in the Mortuary and turned my gaze on the stasis chamber. I opened the seal door but left the stasis field intact to make sure that there was no degradation in the conditions of the bodies held therein. I could not enter the chamber but I could view it clearly as the mist drifted through the air, keeping their bodies perfectly preserved for later examination. I started with a large canvas to capture all three of them together but it felt wrong and so swapped for two small ones; one focusing on Leon and the other for Gareth and Lucile.

I had rendered a great likeness of Lucile already but as I started to strike lines across my blue wash it dawned on me that it wasn't all of the figures that I needed to capture, just a snap shot of the pair, and so I sat and stared at them. I looked at those two copulating figures for an hour, letting my eyes drift wherever they wished to most till I set upon an area that I knew summed up all my questions, and thoughts, and feelings for the couple. I went off and got a coffee and then returned to make sure. As soon as I saw them I knew I was on the right lines and so a fresh canvas went onto the easel and I started again.

A very light blue wash was applied to the canvas and I sat and waited for it to dry while I studied the lines, the textures, the lengths and worked out how close I wanted to close in. I measured from range and noted on a small e-pad and generally busied myself till I could not resist any longer and so flashed into action.

I decided I needed to capture Gareth and Lucile's bodies from the tops of their shoulders down to their midriffs with one painting and then from the top of Gareth's hips to mid way down his thighs, Lucile's legs wrapping around him, her hand clutching desperately at his muscular buttocks with the second.

I worked the paint to get the right colours, the right shapes and swinging lines, the tension in the muscles, the frozen moment in the middle of frantic action. I could feel pleasing warmth spread through me as I knew this was the way to start my journey and as the work took shape I became more and more aroused as Lucile's voluptuous figure came to fill my canvas; Gareth's powerful arms and shoulders taut, the muscles on his back engorged with blood as he fed on her sexuality, Lucile arching backwards, displaying everything she had to offer him as they rutted vigorously.

It wasn't the fact that they were empty vessels that was peaking my imagination and having this unforeseen affect on me, their transformations were not pleasing to me in any way. I liked them both and had been intimate with Lucile so for them to be gone was a tragedy. No, their bodies were not arousing; it was the act that was arousing. This, an act of passion, acted out in public but never intended to be seen, and yet there in front of me and captured in great detail. It was private and yet I was here, viewing their naked bodies entwined. It was voyeuristic and I was painting them, creating my own image of their act.

I put my brush down and moved around to a different vantage point so that instead of standing side on to them I was now standing more behind them. From here I could capture Gareth and Lucile's powerful legs but more importantly her hand, fingers splayed across his buttock, pulling him into her. I washed my next canvas and then the alarm sounded telling me me it was time for dinner.

I obeyed the alarm as I had taught myself to, shut the door to the stasis chamber, washed out my brushes and left the easels where they were in the mortuary. They looked like reporters or photographers, standing outside a celebrity's window, stealing an image of an illicit act.

Dinner was a complicated affair as I had selected several courses to give myself a treat, Lucile sat in the kitchen and oversaw me as I had watched her earlier. I was curious as to what she was thinking and so knew it was time to ask some probing questions that only she could give me the answers to.

'Why so blatant Lucile? Why did you feel the need to copulate like that?'

She watched me but gave away nothing. I decided it was fair to suppose answers and presume that she would argue if I was slanderously wrong or perhaps insulting.

'I think you were bored with the mission and had been consorting with Gareth for some time,' I sneaked a look at her but she stayed still as though she had no idea what I was talking about.

'You needed excitement and Leon was dependable and very kind but ultimately not exciting... Much like me.' She stayed silent while I cooked and talked, 'and so you did something wild with him at a dangerous time, in an inappropriate place, because neither of the people on the Buckingham that you have copulated with would've joined you in the activity.'

'We were too controlled,' I switched off the oven and started to serve the meal and gather my drink as I continued to probe her.

'So you had decided to do this before you entered the room; you had probably been copulating with Gareth for a while before but you urged him to enter you and as he did the passion made you careless, because living on the Buckingham was too safe for you in general.' I was on to something and I knew it so I sat up on the work surface and ate there, disappointing my dinner guest no end by pulling an impromptu no show. It was something totally out of character for the woman who always arrived early to make sure she was never late.

'You loved the attention and you loved the recklessness of the act and it was something that you had tasted before; the way you have your head cast back, soaking every sensation, every touch, indicates to me that you know how to gain the most from your partner; enjoying the moment to the fullest.' Steam swam in the air, drifting up from my plate luxuriously.

'You loved his passion and so when that tiny alarm sounded when you put your hand down, so you could drive your hips harder against his you probably didn't even notice, and if you had you couldn't have predicted the minor technical faults that led to the cascade reaction. You almost certainly didn't care until it was too late and even then the venting froze you so quickly that there would have been no pain or sensation at all really.'

I picked through my first course and then filled my plate. Again I looked through the doorway and saw the other paintings waiting in silence but I knew they didn't mind, after all they weren't people, just my painted companions.

'I think what I want to know is this; why was I never enough to inspire that feeling? That need in you? I don't think it bothers me massively but I would like to know. Was I uninspiring while in union? Surely there was something that drew you to me in the month we were together? Or was it just my desire for you?'

I tried to remember how we had found ourselves in union and found that I remembered her asking me about my relationship with David. I had taken this to be an invitation veiled as a question; to ascertain if I was available. I told her I was and that I was interested in pursuing a union with her. Was I mistaken? Had she been after David? Was I nothing more than convenient?

'You said you wanted a union with me because of my passion. I remember you telling me I had touched you with my work, that my artist's eye aroused you. Oh...' I came to a memory of us standing naked in her quarters, looking at my latest creation; a rogue asteroid with its vapour trail and spinning debris that we had logged while scanning the space we travelled through.

She had stood there and asked where I found the illusion of depth and I had explained how using light, colour and contrast formed the illusion that allowed it to fool the eye and that I poured my heart into finding those colours and thinking about the direction the debris was spinning. It made me realise that even something as dead as this object could still give the illusion of life and drama. She hugged me there in front of the painting and soon after we deunified.

Could she have viewed me as I had that rock? Spinning, active, capable of touching many when really taking away the colour and light it is just dead inside, devoid of real passion or character? Could that be why I split from her, and David for that matter, and perhaps that was even the reason that they were so happy to remain friends and watch from afar while not getting so close as to realize that I was incapable of real emotional depth?

I left the plate at my side and slid down, walking quickly past Lucile I entered the Dining room. I hunted down David and looked at his face as he sat in his chair and I wanted him to tell me it wasn't so, yet when I saw his eyes, the eyes I knew, the eyes I had depicted, I saw sadness and maybe the hint of pity. Pity for whom? Sadness at the ending of our union or that he wasn't able to help me further?

We had spilt on my behest and it had been amicable but I thought about those last few days and realised he had not shown a great desire to copulate with me but instead seemed far more interested in getting me to talk . He wanted me to open up and show him what I was thinking and when I found that difficult we would break from conversation and then resume after we had sat together in silence for a while. He wasn't needy or invasive; he was just trying to get me to open up, like he would if I were one of his patients.

Was that how he thought of me? Was that what I was?!

I became angry at him and Lucile and normally I would simply walk away and fume, or 'redirect' my energy elsewhere (normally into my work) but not this time. It wheeled up inside me till it spilt out of my mouth in a torrent of abuse directed at David. I told him he was boring and uninspiring and that I didn't need his help! That I would never need to 'prove' I was alive or passionate about life and all it offered! I had suffered for my art! I had pursued its release! I HAD LAID MYSELF BARE ON CANVAS!

I don't know how long I ranted but I became tired, almost overwhelmingly upset and I cried. I cried in front of David as I never would in real life and the others saw me sob on the floor and beat my fists against the table.

This release, this truth, had hurt me and I didn't need to force myself to leave the room in a controlled fashion, they had seen it all come apart for the briefest of times and so I was humble and apologised for the scene and went to bed. I didn't wash, I just curled up on the bed after kicking the two dummies over the sides and I went to sleep.

In the morning I realised the honeymoon period of the trip was finished and that I would have to be careful from now on to keep myself together. That night the panther had returned. She stood above me, pinning me to the dirt, saliva dripping from her mouth onto my neck and face. I sobbed uncontrollably as she lingered there, inescapable, unflinchingly looking down at me, aware that I was completely in her power.

CHAPTER SIXTEEN

TOUGHEN UP

The alarm woke me the next morning and I found it hard to get out of bed, as though I had been drained of energy while I slept, and yet still I did rise and do what I needed to. I completed all the checks and prepared for the run, knowing breakfast called before I could set off.

I entered the kitchen and realised that I hadn't tidied up from the night before. I bypassed the table with all those judging faces and packed all the dishes and pots into the cleaner. Lucile was still by the doorway, her face capturing the gratification of her union with Gareth and I stopped, realising it didn't bother me as much as I thought it would do.

Was it that she was transformed and so I would not have to face her? No. Was it that I was better than her? No. Perhaps it was that in the light of my own revelations I had found peace? That as bad as the notion of pity from others was at least it told me something; it told me that I was closed to others, that perhaps the problem was not hers and David's (and to think of it Ben's) but mine?

I know I am not easy to live with, that people find my silence and contained emotions difficult to cope with but it's not easy or natural for me to relax as other people do. I have had to be controlled for so long, felt that I needed to be the adult, even as a child, that it seems to be all I know. While growing up I felt the need to rise above my parent's childish attempts to make the other one jealous so how was I supposed to change now? I didn't need to change was the logical answer. I needed to retain that which made me unique, the thing Jesubrahmed tells us to always protect and nurture; our spirit, our soul. After all, this spirit; this soul, backed by my control, had brought me through many tough times and hard choices and they had always made a difference in my life. I had endured hardship and come out stronger each time. I had evolved. Was this what I was doing unconsciously now? Adapting to survive? Keying into my emotions, buried deep with good reason, to let me loose enough control to retain my sanity?

It was perplexing but I found I was able to work through this process, thinking and looking at their faces while I wiped tables and surfaces and then completed my checks. Today though I didn't stay looking into the cryogenic sections or stray into the mortuary, no, my body was demanding something from me. I carried the nervous energy all the way to the bridge and checked the oxygen levels, air filtration systems and universal buoy.

All three were in order as always and so I went straight past section eight and gathered my running equipment, selected the course I was to complete and slashed two minutes off the self imposed time I had to complete it in. Why just maintain an engine when you can improve it? I set off at breakneck pace and hammered through the corridors, the ship took each footfall and amplified it, making them announce my presence to all in the Buckingham, sleeping, transformed, predatory jungle cat hiding in the recesses of mind; all knew I was stepping up my program and that I was a force to reckoned with on this day and all others that would follow it. The impacts of my feet couldn't have been any louder than normal, and yet each footfall felt thunderous, breaching the still centre of my companion; The Buckingham.

Up ladders, and ramps, down corridors and through doorways changing direction as quickly as I could, sweat pouring from my light brown skin making me stink. I slipped once or twice and caught myself before I hit the floor or the wall and normally I would go back and check that the deck was not faulty but today I just hammered onwards, determined to break the time I had set for myself.

I pushed through the pain barrier as I normally did but it was more visceral, more urgent. It was harder and yet when I came crashing through the finish line back at the dining room I felt better than normal. I was tired, out of breath and my legs were shaking. I sat down but instead of seeking out a chair I slumped against the wall and slid down to the floor. I checked my time knowing it was faster than normal and couldn't believe my personal monitor telling me I had completed the course four minutes faster than normal! It was a massive difference!

I checked the data and found it to be correct and I knew that if I was willing to push myself I could go much faster than my standard times. I knew I would have to find challenging runs from now on, of course mixed with the upkeep ones, but I had felt the animal running with me around the ship and I liked the fact that it was out of the cage, even if it was only for special occasions.

Deck eight called to me and I entered to find that the faces I had painted were technically excellent and conveyed the emotion that I had wanted them to, so if I could bring their faces to life then what was to stop me from making the change in my own existence and become more emotional myself? Nothing, and yet everything as of course I would have to teach myself and I was the one with the control issues. Yet had I not already started my own therapy? Had I not already found problems and found solutions for them, ways of dealing with or confronting them that produced positive outcomes? I was not negative, depressed or incapable; I just needed to be more capable, more proactive and surer that showing emotion was not showing weakness. It could be seen as showing my strength.

I walked out of deck eight and took myself to dinner, I didn't talk to the guests but I didn't avoid them either. Ben, mother, father and David all sat where they normally did with Lucile spying from the kitchen. I ate a simple pasta dish, rich with tomatoes and basil and then spent ten minutes contemplating the cupboard. Ivan and Salvador hadn't come out of there in a couple of days and though I had no love for either of them I couldn't keep them in the cupboard just because I didn't like them.

Ivan had been a minor irritation, more indicative of the sort of person who judged me for who they thought I was before even getting to the truth; that I was what others would classify as cold. He was dismissible because he hadn't had that much impact, but Salvador? Salvador needed to come out so I could have it out with him properly once and for all. No longer would I be content to annoy him by eating in front of him or scribbling with a pencil, now I would plan his downfall, but it would wait until I was ready for him.

*

The weeks passed and time drifted by as Salvador stayed in the cupboard. If I had allowed David and Lucile to upset me Salvador was the kind of encounter that would have me flooding the ship with oxygen and setting a match a blaze. The idea twisted itself in a knot in my head and I realised that I could indeed do such a thing, but due to security and safety protocols only one deck could be flooded in such a way and I would have to use the terminal with-in the flooded deck to activate the process. I would have to do it in an enclosed space and be standing in it when it lit. Theoretically the pain wouldn't last long as my body would be scorched within a matter of seconds, though it would probably be a horrible transformation, not quick like hanging or perhaps a long drop from one of the cargo containers in the hold.

I found my hard physical exercise had brought me a manner of peace and I could see the change in my body now, the muscles becoming more defined and I was losing some weight, nothing major, just pounds. I looked tougher and more robust and I was pleased with the benefits of the regime, the extra energy, stronger limbs and harder lines around my body.

Sleeping for more than six hours at a stretch became difficult so I came to the conclusion that staying up later was not really the option I wanted to go for. Instead I would come home and eat and be asleep by ten and so rising at three or four o clock in the morning. The ship's systems were constant and so it mattered not what time I was awake as the same amount of noise and activity would be going on, and yet I found it made a difference to me. At four in the morning I knew others would be sleeping and so I was quiet. I would get up, dress, grab stasis fruit from the kitchen and then walk the halls.

Grey and lifeless the ship seemed to be sleeping as normal, sane people would be, as I should have been and yet was not. I felt like I was observing the ship without its knowledge, like a voyeur I stroked its walls and peered through the plastics to see the empty labs and equipment in storage. I watched the oriental woman sleep in cryo and wondered if she was aware I was there. I would sit in front of her and want to wake her; to see what she was like, how her voice really sounded, what she smelt like.

The alarm would chime and I would rise to go and get a proper breakfast before my gruelling running, climbing and weights session, then on to deck eight where I was coming close to completion. The walls were now lined with people who wore their generic tight grey jumpsuits and stared out at me as I painted but they were broken up by the colourful individuals that I had injected into their ranks, the ones that reflected that the colonists were all individuals working towards a collective goal.

I took all of the paintings I completed and placed them on deck eight where they sat on specially constructed stands made of Graphene sheets. The days pulled along until finally I was so close to being done that I felt a wave of euphoria wash through me as I walked past the painted walls. It was an achievement of some note and one that really did need to be seen to be believed. In many ways I had brought the colonists to life through an amalgamation of my art and the computers image projection systems. It was modern and yet traditional, clever yet simple, striking in places designed to break up the ordinary and yet it showed the collective. Wherever I stood I thought it looked amazing.

This was a project I had entered into without prompting, something I had designed, planned and made myself and I was proud of the achievement, but something was slightly troubling about the end of this artistic journey, something that was inevitable; it was coming to an end. The space had been filled and the areas of interest that I had wanted to capture, bar two rooms, were done. Two spaces lay blank and empty on the deck, spaces reserved for the pieces depicting the dining room and the Core Support Room.

Easels still sat in the mortuary with Lucile and Gareth's image upon it. The other pieces simply defied capture. I couldn't even get paint on canvas in the dining room, let alone bring its likeness through my brushes. These rooms seemed to taunt me and as the final pick up alterations and adjustments were being made I found the two empty seats on the stands even harder to look at. What would I need to do to bring them to me, to access them emotionally? I didn't know, though I believed that perhaps they were locked for a reason, like a pyromaniac is kept from incendiary devices to protect themselves and others perhaps I was being kept from discovering the truth about those spaces?

The answer was not forth coming but soon I would have even bigger problems. I was entering my seventh month, that was when the others were meant to return but there had been no activity on the bridge computers, indicating that no one was in range to uplink from the rescue ship. I ran diagnostics but knew our short and long range sensors were working so they simply weren't out there yet.

In truth I could see danger on the horizon and so drew plans to battle it. I was going to survive this because I was mentally tough enough and that was all there was to it, I would survive at any and all costs.

CHAPTER SEVENTEEN

ONE DOOR CLOSES AND ANOTHER ONE OPENS

I could feel the pressure building in my head, the greater feeling of tension, bringing on nausea and confusion. I checked all the gages and temperatures, gas monitors and cryogenic systems four times, making sure; being meticulous for the safety of the ship, for the colonists, for me personally, is what I was telling myself but I was actually procrastinating.

All my life I have forged ahead, taking steps to make sure I had a goal, a plan; something to reach for, yet now that was all slipping away. Deck eight was nearly complete, in fact all that I really needed to do was remove the supplies and tweak the directions of a few stands and it was done. I knew I had finished and also knew that once done I could never fool myself into thinking more needed doing. If it was complete then it was complete... And deck eight was complete.

I walked through the corridors slowly, trying to stop myself from dragging my feet but failing miserably, and yet not being able to resist chastising myself for not hurrying. I had made up my mind that once finished I would close the section off and seal it so that I could not influence it later on. I wanted it to be a pure record and reflection of my time alone on the Buckingham and had selected something that would take me many months to complete. It had been in production for seven months and twenty two days and now it was finished. I just had to get my equipment out and seal it.

The doors slid open and revealed the space I had created, a sea of people, thousands projected onto the walls using millimetre thick image display rolls made of Graphene sheets. Every five feet a member of the crew had been highlighted, painted in their favoured clothing and colours as they stood surrounded by their fellow colonists wearing tight, grey jumpsuits. They were individuals and I was the one who had brought them to the front, not because they were better than any of the other colonists, but just because they stood out to me.

The main room was where I placed my other works, with no free standing display space left unaccounted for. The two gaps that I could not fill with depictions of the dining room and the Core Control room I had filled with two alternative paintings. The first was a depiction of one of the cryogenic bays; the colonists clearly viewable through the clear fronted cryo-tubes. They were all wearing their grey, skin tight stasis suits, sleeping in perfect hibernation. Below them I had painted a shadow, cast by someone walking past, though the shadows owner could not be seen. It was my shadow, cast by my body. It was me.

I was the ghost that watched them but was never seen.

The second was a personal piece. I took images of our destination in high summer, taken by the probes that first investigated our new planet and confirmed it was habitable, and painted the rolling Purple and orange vegetation and the blue skies above that were soft and beautiful. Even more beautiful was the female colonist, running through a high meadow, wearing a floral dress and smiling. She was more radiant than the scenery, the colours of her white dress with blossom print practically glowed and she herself seemed to be the perfect woman, her clear physical capability not detracting from her feminine grace and incredible beauty. Her eyes were deep and her lips rich and textured, parted slightly as she breathed deeply due to the exertion of running through the paradise she was framed in. My muse from the wall depicted as the embodiment of hope and success in the new world we would find ourselves on.

It was a personal piece and I have never liked a painting of mine more. Of course the rose lovers drew a reaction from my parents but this image? It drew one from me.

I basked in its glory, the sweeping colours, the researched plants and the strange but familiar sky, her movement through the scene captured with the breeze blowing her long black hair away from her face, the light, more intense than Homeworlds, bathing her in gold. She looked like a Goddess and I had never been so proud of a painting of mine before in my life. It was as though a little of her soul shone out through her skin, more beautiful than the most sweeping of landscapes.

Of course this wasn't the light of her soul. This wasn't the purity of her being that was glowing on canvas, it was mine. I had painted her as I envisioned her, with all my hopes for her life and the lives of my fellow colonist, my soul transported into her, her life seen through my eyes.

It was deeper than soul, greater than love, more uplifting than hope... It was the God in us all revealed through my brush, my colours, my vision and my skill... It was my ascension. My moment of truth and pure clarity, as Jesubrahmed would have said. I had found the piece of deity that resided in all of us, I had recognised it and I had shown it my acceptance and love. I had found God inside me and God had I so become.

I stepped back and away from that painting and knew there was a chance I would not see it again, yet still I had to do what I had planned from the start; what I must do to protect my work. I stepped back and out of the door, the light from the room flooding over me as I stood in the comparatively dark corridor looking in. My eyes never left her; never moved from her form. I stood there for a full two minutes, watching her, drinking in the image before finally I shut the door and locked it.

I inputted my command code and set the door lock to encrypt, allowing it to only be opened by someone with Alpha clearance. Once initialized I wouldn't be able to get in to deck eight no matter what I did and it would remain sealed as it was until a custodial captain or colony leader requested clearance to enter the deck.

I pressed the confirm button on my touch screen and sat down opposite the door in the corridor, I felt the magnetic lock drop into place as the hairs on the back of my neck stood up. I was free of deck eight forever now. It was done. Like the day I had walked away from Salvador's I felt both sick inside and yet relieved it was over. Scared of what the future held for me and yet then I had had a plan, a place to go, a starting point to begin anew. Here I had just the ship. Just the ship.

*

That day I spent moving my paints, easels and brushes to the only other space I had to work with; deck fourteen. I had started by leaving it all outside in the corridor, just sitting outside the deck, but I couldn't just leave it strewn in the way, it had to have a place; we all have a place in the universe. I believe we all have a calling, all have something we need to do; something we are meant to do.

Jesubrahmed said that you would know if what you were doing was right if you felt it in your heart. You would feel your calling, and be at peace, no matter what the universe asked you to be. If calmness and reason were your allies, peace would be with you, in you, no matter how chaotic the world around you became. When I looked at the painting of my running muse and knew it was I who had brought it forth I knew I was doing what I needed to do; what I was born to do.

My thoughts returned not to Jesubrahmed and his teachings but to Salvador and his prejudices. Could I have still enough fear of him to be avoiding him here, light-years away from Homeworld and his presence... And yet I felt him in the cupboard some nights. Knew he was there, judging me.

I stepped through the doorway of deck fourteen and found a corridor before me. The one I had programmed so long ago. It had doors coming off it, every ten feet or so and those rooms were bright and the walls were blazing with their blank, challenging, clean, pure emptiness. It screamed out to me to be painted, to be adapted and personalised and altered and made to fit my will and view. Yet I looked at the walls and could imagine nothing on them bar their white glow.

The equipment I put in the first room, adding to the supplies I had placed in there over seven months ago. There was more than enough space and more than enough deck settings to challenge me for months to come and yet nothing wanted to be done in this space. It was as though it was as blank as my immediate future.

I walked as far as two doors down and then stopped, my P.S.M.P told me the dimensions of the other rooms and that they were all identical bar the end room which was larger than the rest by a factor of almost two. I looked down towards that end room but it seemed so far away and the walls and ceiling and floor were so bright that I didn't want to go any further. I could have adjusted the settings on the deck but I didn't. I didn't feel I had the right to. Something about this place stood before me, like an immovable object and I could not simply press a button and eradicate it. I would have to tame it, hone it, and make it bend to my creative will. But how?

I walked back to the door and sat down. The light surrounded me, emitted from the graphene laced sensors that carried a charge better than any other substance humanity knew of. The light enveloped me as I pulled fruit from the satchel I carried with me and I ate. I ate my lunch and drank from my flask and watched those blank walls as I tried to battle the contrast of emotions now smothering me. The euphoria of knowing deck eight was finished and locked, ready to be discovered by the colonist and crew, against the fear and confusion of not knowing what I was doing or where I was going. There was no plan here now, no contingency I could think of. This space was mine to use and yet I felt I could not fill it. Was I empty? Had the running woman stolen the last ounce of my artistic urge and left me alone and scared in the light?

I discounted that notion straight away and demanded a higher standard of panicked thought from that point on. I spoke to myself sternly, laying it out like it was. I had a space to transform and I had time to do it in. If the worst came to the worst I would paint the ship and scenes from it and place the canvases in storage in the rooms. This could be a library for my work, or a place to store supplies, with each room playing host to a different colour.

I stood and forced myself to access the deck controls. I looked through them but could not see an alternative layout that captured me at all and so I decided to keep the corridor but move it so that there were several turns in it, like the world's most unimaginative maze or perhaps the universes brightest Labyrinth, for there was no way to turn and become lost, this corridor only ever led down to one place; the room at the end that I could not bare to enter. I eradicated half the rooms and thinned the corridors to give me the panels needed to take my sharp right and left angled turns, to make a twisting path that took me, inevitably to the large room at the end. I then looked at the settings and I turned the light down so that the walls, ceiling and floors exuded light but did not blind like before. Finally I altered the texture of the walls; giving them a rough finish perfect for my paint to stick on to.

The alarm sounded as I looked at the corridor that was now only three and a half feet wide compared to the standard five it had been before and I knew I had started something. I had no idea what it was but I knew that deck fourteen now had a beginning. That logically indicated a middle and an end too. It was no longer a blank canvas, the wash was on and all I needed to do was realize a vision.

CHAPTER EIGHTEEN

SALVADOR

I took my leave of my parent's house the day after my sixteenth birthday. I didn't want a party or any real celebration but instead had a quiet dinner with mother and father, at their request, at a restaurant of their choosing. Upon returning home I reminded them I would be off in the morning and that I would probably be leaving early so I could have breakfast in my new apartment. I'd had all of my possessions removed from the my parents house on my birthday and the new furniture delivered and managed by a man I'd hired to oversee the project so the only thing left to move was me. They took it as well as could be expected. Mother decided to go out for some 'essentials' and would be gone for an hour or so while father told me he loved me and was proud of my individuality and then retired to his office to work on some colonial plans.

I may as well have been alone in the house, pretty much as I had been for the last four years, as both of them were so caught up in their lives and the task of avoiding spending time together that I'd become something to avoid as well. Later on, after I left, they reconciled and moved to that happy state of ignoring what the other one was up to no matter how blatant it was. I remember my mother slipping out to get something from the kitchen while hosting a party years later. She was gone a long time. She returned with coffee, mints and biscuits for us and our guests saying it was difficult to find them and that the kitchen staff were too busy to satisfy her properly. Bizarrely struck by the sort of curiosity that I normally reserved for a subject I was about to paint I took myself off to the toilet and checked downstairs.

The male cook was busy drinking a glass of champagne as he relaxed on a chair in the kitchen. His shirt was undone and I could see my mother's flame red lipstick emblazoned on his chest and neck, his belt was open and the base of his penis disappearing into his undone trousers. He looked up at me and saw me staring at him. He was an attractive man even for the modern human that was so well groomed and exercised.

He issued me down into the kitchen and smiled at me seductively and I considered going, not because of how attractive he was but because I was sure it would annoy my mother. I took a step down and was saved from a carnal act of revenge as my mother entered the room from the other door. I slipped quickly up the steps and watched her cross the room having not seen me and stoop down in front of his chair. She placed her hand on his groin as she stood up holding her knickers. She hitched her skirt up showing him exactly what she was about to cover with the undergarments and presumably what he would be seeing again very soon.

Mother straightened her dress, leaned in and kissed him and then told him to 'fucking get dressed.' I watched her walk out and looked back to see the cook smile at me and issue me forward again with his hands. I shook my head and went up the stairs and back to the party. Father met me as I walked in and hugged me as though I wasn't a disappointment to him; the sort of affection rarely shown to me when not in polite company.

'Merry Christmas Gita,' he said smiling and then walked off to talk to one of the other forty guests that they had in their mansion. The ground floor was nearly all open planned allowing them to hold these large parties without fear of the guests wandering around the house and uncovering their secrets. Mother stalked around the room like a vixen waiting to pounce on an unsuspecting chicken, skirting conversations and laughing with those she past until she breezed up behind me.

'You should have stayed in the kitchen dear, far more exciting down there I can tell you.' She walked away grinning and took the arm of a man that I knew to be a famous artist. They chatted and stood very closely as my father spoke to a statuesque, blond woman in the corner that worked for him setting up colonies and winning contracts. It was all such a pointless dance and one that sickened me so much that I had to turn away. Standing beside me was the famous and much loved Terrance Woogian. He winked at me and smiled deeply.

'Hello Gita, do you remember me?' He asked, his face the same as it had been that day when I was nine and he had made me feel like I was worth something for a change.

'How could I forget Mr Woogian. You look well.' It was a polite answer and truthful, for we all looked well and yet there was something missing from him now. He seemed shorter and the spark in the eyes that I had seen years ago was merely a dying flicker now.

'I am well, though, and do not take me to be ungrateful, I have tired of these engagements,' the spark returned for a second. It was as though telling the truth reinvigorated him for a short time.

'I myself was about to go, but I stay for them,' I indicated in the direction of my parents. He nodded understanding and tipped his half empty glass towards them.

'How are they? Still carrying on?'

'Yes,' was all I could muster on the subject. If he knew enough to know this was just a projection of their lives and not the reality then he knew that discussing the status of their relationship was pointless. 'How are you Mr Woogian? What brings you here?'

'Well I followed my agent who is networking for a tour he's planning for me. It turns out that I am still popular, though not 'rapid' enough to be 'an event' anymore. I'm in possession of an act that everyone has seen.' He smiled and looked around the room at the guests mingling.

'That doesn't diminish its value if you are still performing it well,' I answered taking stock of the room as was he. I saw famous faces, models and sportsmen, industrialists and singers; they swarmed around each other like parasitic insects, feeding off each other's fame and notoriety. We stood together and though we seemed the odd ones out I felt that at that time we were the most normal people in the room.

Woogian touched my arm and leaned towards me, completely at ease with his intrusion into my personal space I leaned in to listen to what he was saying above the din of fake laughter and the clinking of glasses filled with Dutch courage.

'I can honestly say I have never forgotten your wonderful art or how intelligent you struck me as being at such a young age. May I introduce you to someone that I believe could help you? Would that be considered forward or perhaps meddling? Clearly you are not a woman who would have others command her choices.' He turned to face me as he said this so that his lips were very close to mine. He was not attractive to me but his honesty was and for the briefest of seconds I felt the urge to kiss him. It passed as he pulled back and looked me in the eyes. I nodded my approval and Woogian slipped away into the crowd.

I watched him walk over to my mother and engage her and the artist she was with in conversation. Woogian asked her something and she told him she would be 'right back' and slipped away towards my father. As soon as she left he turned to the artist and spoke to him quickly, they were smiling at each other and then looked towards me. I of course made sure that I looked away as though I had been scanning the crowd for someone else. Woogian smiled at my mother as she returned and the artist made his way towards me. Later that night Woogian would cover my early exit with an impromptu three song set that delighted the crowd. He was a lovely man and I firmly believe he was motivated by the simple wish to aid me.

'Hello, my name is Salvador Iranie... You have heard of me yes?' He had a strange mix of accents, part Spanish and part American, and his words came out slightly slurred as he had been drinking. I knew of him and I loved his work, he had a flair for the dramatic and was a controversial figure in the artistry world. Many believed him to be a genius that suffered from insecurities and personality flaws that gave him the passion and energy needed to produce the work he did. He was the leader of the 'No God' movement and his art and spite were nearly always directed towards the 'hypocrisy' of Jesubrahmed. It wasn't a sentiment I shared but I could never ignore the brilliance of his vision or his ability to adapt over the years to changing fashions.

He didn't sell much work but what he did sell went to private collectors for fortunes. He wasn't under threat of religious retribution as the negative aspects of religion and the formalised structure had been stripped away. You could worship anywhere at any time and if others minded it was their lack of faith that disturbed them not the presence of yours.

At this point I was only thirty, had travelled the world and painted some of its wonders and its fine people but had not made a name for myself as I had hoped to. I was well thought of but that was the summit of people's appraisal of my work. 'Give her twenty years and perhaps we will have something of real substance to view from her,' they said, and though I hid it well (as I nearly always did) It still hurt me.

Salvador was before me and for the briefest of minutes I was star struck.

'I know who you are and have seen much of your work,' I replied blushing slightly, aware of my loss of control and irritated it manifested so obviously for all to see.

'Well your mother tells me you would be interested in an apprenticeship with me studying art and Woogian has often told me you are THE rising star.' He said it as though this was the holy-grail to me as though it would stamp a seal of approval on my work to go and study under a famous artist. In truth I wanted to do it on my own. To learn and become who I needed to be without someone else's help.

'I suppose I would be but I am very busy with my own studies already,' I answered starting my gentle climb back from his possible offer.

'This is what your mother said; she told me you would probably want to but be afraid to take such an offer of help. Personally I think she was annoyed because I refused to pleasure her earlier in the gardens but maybe she is right...' Salvador started to turn away from me, not to leave but to cast his eye into the room and stand right next to me.

'I have watched the way you interact with each other, you, your father and mother. It is almost like you are something they are coveting, of course not sexually; but you are the power here. If you wanted to you could stop all this with a wave of your hand, but you don't, so they spiral around you flashing their feathers and singing their songs because they want you to see how desirable they are, how masterful, how powerful.'

He sipped his drink and smiled as mother looked back at us and smiled broadly, as though she was so clever to know we would stand but never leave together, that we were incompatible and she was perhaps showing me the difference between a great artist like Salvador and one who simply paints; namely me. I smiled back and looked at Salvador closely; he found my attention almost irritating and sneered at me.

'What are you staring at woman?'

'You... Do you want an apprentice or is this all chatter to fill the room?' I was blunt; it would turn out to be how our relationship would always be.

'I am interested in you but are you prepared to stay with me for a fixed period? I do not select apprentices lightly. I have seen your work and you are quite good but my name carries much weight and that weight would give you power, so we must be clear that you would stay to learn.'

'I will stay to learn but I will not be your skivvy, or your slave. I won't lay on my back for you and I do not prostrate myself at anyone's feet. If you want an apprentice who is working towards being your equal then I am interested, if you want an adoring fool who'll climb onto all fours for you then we need not talk anymore,' I shot back calmly. Salvador watched my father and mother circle the party and finished his champagne, his predominantly Spanish stock clear in the racial markers of his skin and face.

'You will learn and I will teach but never can there be any 'relationship' between us. I am a master of the arts and you will be my student, my pupil,' he turned to face me obviously irritated that I wasn't swooning under his charm or celebrity status.

'You see me as a work in progress no doubt and I would have to earn your respect I take it?'

'If you are able to do so then yes, though I have never seen a princess who has real soul; real understanding,' I looked into his eyes and saw something dark lurking there, but I dismissed it as just the champagne's effect upon him.

'Then you have never met me before, but you have now. Congratulations, you have a new apprentice,' I stated and took the glass he was holding off of him and handed him a full one as the waitress brought a full tray past.

'I will stay with you for eighteen months,' I said as he bolted his drink back far quicker than he had the last. 'And you will teach me all that there is for me to learn or start me on the right way.'

We looked at each other and nodded and it was done. The next day I went with him to the union of Brazil where I would spent the next eighteen accursed months. People have said that my mother wept when she found out I had gone to stay with Salvador and so she should have, for he was a cruel and brutal man.

*

Will I tell you everything he did to me? How he was every day? No. It is a part of my life I am not proud of, a time when I lost sight of who I was and became something lesser, someone weaker than I should be. I know I am stronger than the wretch he abused.

Then there is the truth, and the truth is that I feel ashamed when I think of that time. Ashamed that I allowed myself to be used and downtrodden and that he got to me so quickly, removed my power and kept me suffocating for so long. It hurts that I let him do that to me. It hurts that she let him do that to me.

You see the truth is that no-one really believed I had the pedigree to be the artist I wanted to be, no-one close to me believed what I was doing was going to be a success or that I should be doing it at all. They wanted me to fail and they wanted to show me how weak I really was... And the truth is that it worked.

What do I fear about that time that still hurts me now? Why does it still haunt me? Why do I hate as I never have before? Why do I fear when all I really have to do is remember and accept what happened?

I tell you that I always move forward, that I always have a plan, that I always know where I'm going and that the past means little to me, but the longer I stayed alone on The Buckingham the more I understood the reality of my being; I do not look back because I feel the breath of my enemy on my neck, I do not look back for fear I will fall and be devoured by the panther that chases me.

That damned panther.

So I will tell you of Salvador, how he was and how he could be and how he hated me. How we arrived and he took me to his small mansion in Brazil in the 'La Canela' quarter which stood high on the hills above Rio De Janeiro. It was once the slum area that became world famous until Brazil exploded onto the world as the leading economy of the twenty first century. It held its hand high ever after that, even managing to become one of the first areas to embrace Jesubrahmed as the new messenger of God, in so doing bypassing the bitter years of in fighting and skirmishes that plagued the once rich Middle East.

His mansion was simple and small compared to many around him and yet it was far more tasteful and known for being one of the best, a melding of old design and new materials that led to his building being almost entirely made out of Graphene sheeting and plastic polymers. It looked almost normal from the outside as he had programmed every inch of the mansion to make the sheets conform to the textures and shapes of normal tiles, bricks and mortar. But with a press of a button the house could become translucent, alter its outer visage or even change the interior structure as the building was held together with electrical signals and locking systems that protected the building in case of power cut.

It was one of the first of its kind and one of the reasons I could make the decks allotted to me do what I wanted them to. I had used the basic technology before.

Salvador was a man with two personalities, two faces, one that he would take out with him and one that he would have behind closed doors. Rumours always flew about how nasty he could be but I simply put it down to jealously. A simple mistake to make but one that I would come to regret (no matter how many times I say I don't, I've come to understand that I do).

When we arrived that morning he told me he had allowed for eighteen months of study and work and that he would see me grow, but within two weeks it was clear this was not going to be as I had envisaged it.

For those first two weeks we discussed art and he would argue with me but he would not lose his temper, he would tell me that I was young or that I could not know as I had not seen many of the things he had. I explained I had been around the world seeing the scars of the religious conflicts, I saw hope for the future in the land returned to arable farming, the reclaimed cities that had been swallowed by the jungles once more, the abundance for those left on Homeworld. I painted hallowed sites and natural wonders and I told him I had captured their beauty but he dismissed this as a boast and told me that I knew little to nothing about the real world and its people, about love and life, about loss and pain, 'You need to experience them before you can be a true artist,' he would tell me while sneering at my privileged upbringing.

At the beginning of the third week he threw out his cleaner and told me that I was to take her place, that part of my experience was to learn humility. I argued but he told me I was weak and had lied about my want to be taken seriously, I countered by saying I was an artist and not a cleaner, he told me I thought I was better than other people because cleaning was beneath me. I tried to reason but he refused to see my point of view, denied it had any weight or credibility and called me a 'princess'.

After a week of neither of us cleaning or picking anything up I assumed the role of cleaner. When he came home from a day of drinking at a friend's domicile he laughed at me for breaking and told me it proved I was weak. I wanted to fight him but I knew he would not budge. I kept cleaning and he would make mess on purpose by pushing over easels or throwing glasses around. He would move the furniture and play loud music at me when I least expected it, he would jump out at me and call me all the names I had ever heard and more. I was his 'mess-whore,' useless apart from that. I could take all of this and more had I been learning properly and discovering the mysteries of art but I wasn't, he had me performing life drawings and landscapes and would rip up my work in front of me and call it weak, useless and soulless. He would attack my work and rip it in two when I was only half way through.

I would toil so I could find the time to paint and then I would face his abuse as he slashed my canvases with knives and broke my brushes under his heel. He banned me from painting with tools for a week and so I used my fingers, he said I was 'predictable' and that 'finger painting' was 'all I was good for'. It was three months before he told me that my mother was coming and that I was to clean the place and make it respectable 'for a queen.' I did as I was told and prayed she would come and see, really see what I was going through, but when she arrived she smiled and looked at the small room I slept in and told me other artists had it far worse. I could see she was not interested in my progress or seeing me at all. She was here in the sun to see him and his friends.

I remember feeling weak, knowing I could just walk out and yet I didn't want him to tell people I had quit, that I couldn't take it, that I wasn't really serious. So I stayed in when they went to dinner and I worked with the new brushes I had bought.

That night they returned drunk and Salvador copulated with my mother in the front room, then upstairs. He shouted at her to scream and show her daughter how to have a good time, to show her passion and she did. She did everything he told her to and in the morning she sat opposite me eating breakfast and smiling. She looked at me and sipped her drink in the sun and asked casually 'do you want to come home Gita?'

I thought about it but it seemed she was tempting me, as though she wanted me to accept my weakness and so I resisted. I shook my head and said 'no.' She looked away and I thought I saw disappointment on her face so I excused myself and I walked away from her to do the cleaning. She watched me for the day and then at night she went with him to his actor friend's house. I would hear later many times how they had enjoyed her like a slut and how she was so much better than me because at least she understood what she was; a whore.

Salvador never touched me sexually; he always said I was beneath him and that I would make him smell of weakness and desperation. He would make me shower with the doors open and if I closed the door he would make the whole house transparent so that I could be seen by anyone overlooking us on those slopes of gold. Sometimes he would bring a woman home and switch the house to its transparent form and copulate with her against my door or would switch on the tannoy system and make me listen. I had no desire to touch him, no desire to do anything with him sexually and he knew that. He did it so he could see the look on my face. So that he could show me his distain.

I would tell you that I pitied him and his insecurities and that he was obviously a flawed and bitter little man but he was also Salvador Irainie, world famous artist and so he had the seal of greatness upon him. I wished to scour it off him but it would still stay there for all to see. He was a master artist and no apprentice was worthy of him.

It took him nine months before his frustration told through and I remember that day clearly. He had been out drinking and returned to a spotless house, silent bar the breathing of his 'mess-whore' who was creating in the kitchen. He walked in and I was in the middle of a painting, one I knew was very good. It was of a woman from the city that I had met that day and invited back so that I could try and capture her divinity. She was beautiful and special, for many reasons. She was old and her skin was wrinkled and weathered from the sun, her teeth were good and she had a smile that offered no real clue as to what she was thinking. Her hair was pulled back and she shone with intelligence and depth. I had captured her uncrowned regal power on the canvas before me. It was all there.

Salvador saw the painting and walked straight past me. He looked at the canvas up close and then stepped back and leaned against the work surface for some time, I don't know how long, but for a long time. He stood there for minutes looking at the paint and then back to the subject and then back again. Finally he smiled at her and spoke to her kindly. He offered her money to get a taxi home but she said she had driven and so he thanked her for being with his apprentice and asked her to return soon so that he too could take his time to paint her as she was so extraordinary.

She left and he watched her electric car pull away. Her lights shining in the darkness as he accessed the house controls, turning the walls as Black as night, the interior lights he left on.

Salvador entered the kitchen and I was convinced he was about to slash the canvas and so stepped forward to stop him. I don't remember how long he beat me or how many times I was even struck but I did find myself on the floor looking up the stairs, watching my painting disappear with him. He returned with his belt and beat me some more and I cannot tell you that I did not plead with him to stop or offer to copulate with him just to make it end. Of course he ignored my pleas and hurt me; not badly enough that I needed medical attention, but he hurt me.

He threw me in my room at the end and told me that he did not want to see me for a day, so that is where I stayed; in my room. Alone. I stayed there and took my sheet off my bed and tried to wipe off the blood. I tried to retain my strength and I knew I could walk away, but I didn't. The next day I came out and did not tidy. Instead I cleaned myself up and ate and then went back to bed and slept.

By day three the house was a tip once more and so I cleaned it and then returned to my studies, only now I would not paint with my fingers or do as he said. Now I would do what I wanted to do for I had seen something in his face I could not understand and needed to see again so that I could learn; so that I could know why he had attacked me and what his attack meant. I would not ask him, I would draw it from him as you would milk a snake of its venom. He would bare his fangs and I would take his spite from him.

It only happened three more times. Three more beatings that I would have avoided at all costs once I was actually sustaining them, yet before

I would bait him. At first it was just with words, leaving his things around on the floor or spitting at him and swearing, but this didn't work. He laughed at me, so I painted as well as I could and still he mocked me but I could see him watching me even though he refused to look at me as I was 'beneath him'. Even though I was banned from eating anywhere other than in my room as I sickened him. Even though I was a princess with no talent I knew I had started to hurt him.

The second beating came when he found me in his room painting his bed; I had captured the frame and the basic details and was in the process of placing in all the figures on the bed lying around him. There were semi and fully nude men and women draped across his naked body; which was accurate in proportion; he was not a well endowed man. They all smiled with their faces turned towards him but their eyes looked away from him at the walls or the ceiling or floor. They were all beautiful and clean and soft and relaxed as opposed to him. He was covered in sweat as though he had been exerting himself greatly but had had little effect on his guests.

I hired all the people locally to be in the painting and they had lain upon his bed as I had asked them to. They were all gone by the time he returned but their image I had committed to digital record and their smell still lingered in the room. Many of them wore expensive perfumes and the air was still sweet after their passing.

It was not my best painting and yet I was proud of it, of course when he saw it he exploded and I saw that look in his eyes again, yes, he was angry but it was more than that. I did not know what but I could see it was there and I was smug for all of a few seconds before my beating began and the pain and fear drove my victory into the darkness. Again he took away the painting and again he returned with the belt. I screamed as he whipped me till blessedly he tired and I finally crawled away from him. He dragged me down the stairs by my hair and tossed me into my room and then struck me twice more with his belt before slamming the door and stamping away.

Each time I would rest a day, banished and alone and I would wonder what it was I had captured? What was that look that marked his face just before he assaulted me?

Every time he attacked he came a little closer to being undone by me. The third beating came from a simple painting of the sunset; I sat capturing the colours with my paints, making long, sweeping brush strokes. The effect was stunning and I stood back to look at it when it was done. Suddenly his hand was in my hair; dragging me off the balcony and down to the floor inside the house. His fists landing cleanly upon me. Another painting gone and another set of strips for my body, earned with paint and passion.

I would capture him the final time he attacked and I'd mark him in return. He was beating me with his belt and I screamed and screamed so loudly that he leapt upon me and held my mouth closed, pressing his fingers over my lips so hard I thought my jaw would break and my teeth would shatter. He pulled at my hair and he banged my face into the Graphene floor so that blood slipped from a cut on my forehead and down my face. He stopped when he saw the blood and I rolled onto my back and drove a broken brush I had been holding into his groin. He screamed and rolled off me and crawled away and I lay on the floor and bled.

I took myself to my room, leaving him lying on the floor whimpering. I came out the next day for medical supplies and he was gone. I cleaned myself up and pulled that sheet off my bed; the sheet I had used to clean myself several times that still bore the red scars of blood stains across it and I placed it in my backpack, the bag went onto my back and I slept with it there until he returned from seeing his doctor.

The front door opened and I walked out of my room, hunched and sore and bruised, but not beaten. He sat down when he saw me and he wept. I watched him as he had watched me; in the back of my mind it occurred to me that I could beat him. I was not weak. I was physically fit and able bar the pain I was suffering and he was bound to be in greater discomfort than I was this time, yet I didn't. I knew what was in his eyes before he attacked me. I had seen him as he really was and knew now why I was here.

The painting I had been working on stood on its easel in the centre of the room. I walked up holding one of the canvas transporting bags he kept in the studio and slipped it into the bag. My back was turned on him but I listened closely for any sound that would indicate movement in case I needed to defend myself.

He didn't move, he just sat sobbing bitterly.

'You are weak and you fear me. You fear me because I see what you cannot. You see what is on the surface, what is obvious, what is mundane where once you saw wonder and depth and life. I know you have had many apprentices here and I know you have taken from them what you have tried to take from me... You took their paintings.'

He looked up at me and through his tears his illusion failed, he was a man, not a master, he was spent, not timeless, he had lost his passion and it could not be brought back to him.

'You have nothing,' I continued, never shouting, never threatening, always even, always in control. 'You will take my paintings, the ones you have not destroyed and you will say that they are yours, that you have spent your time in exile working. You will take my work and display it as your own and whenever someone tells you how amazing you are you will know it is me they are complimenting as it has been the same for the ones before me; your other victims. He didn't try to argue or move; I had seen his lie, his greatest trick and weakness, and knew now he was utterly spent.

'There was a time when you were free and you could see as we do and knew that knowledge was worth hunting, that truth was worth more than any gold, any credit, but now you have no truth and you are spent.' I walked towards the door and he tried to stand but I turned and stared at him until his legs gave way and he slumped back down.

'I will let you show my work as your own. I will let you keep all the money and the fame that you want because I have no need of it. I have a soul and I have a future whereas you are just a ghost, the vessel that once carried the spirit of Salvador Iranie. You are nothing and I know why those that study under you paint as they do. They paint to try and prove they have something that you have not seen, that they can and will beat you, but they always are lesser after being with you because they want to beat you by acquiring more fame and money. To prove to you how weak you are. I will not do that.'

He slipped forwards and spoke up; knowing nothing he said would or could stop me. 'Will you tell them what happened here?'

'No,' I answered with as much strength as I could, though I was tired and felt my fear of the door and of the world outside smother my will. 'I will not paint.'

I walked out and left him. The air was crisp and fragrant and I could feel the breeze on my face. I walked down the path to his gate and out into the world once more, a free woman again, clutching the painting I carried with me tightly.

It had taken me eighteen months, eighteen months to the day to leave and I stayed for what reason? Because I was powerless? Because I was in love with the idea of being Salvador's apprentice? Because I feared he would hurt me? No. I stayed because I would not walk away when my mother knew I had promised to stay for that time. I stayed because I would not allow the world to see I was beaten and that I could not take hardship or pain.

No. I stayed for more than that. I stayed because I was weak. I think I stayed because I was too weak to ask for help when my mother offered it. Because I would not pay the price she demanded. I stayed because I needed to know I was who I said I was and I found out I wasn't.

I wasn't a princess. I wasn't an artist who wanted to be recognised and I wasn't a victim. I found I was someone who would paint because that is what I was meant to do, like a singer who would play to a crowd of one and love it as much as a crowd of ten thousand. I was an artist because I loved to paint, not because I could sell my paintings.

I was a princess and that was something that I took for granted. Something that I always thought meant nothing to others. Perhaps I was wrong about that too?

It took me twenty years to come to a point when I was happy to display my work again. In that time I retired to a quiet life and I worked from my home in the British countryside for my father's company planning programs that would help to bring communities together through art and crafts. I was paid and I was quiet and I was adequate at my job. I loved and settled with Victoria for many years in that time but she left me, left my dull ache and my resolution to be less that I could be by just staying quiet.

Victoria would detest me telling you of our lives together and see it as an intrusion and betrayal on my part. I will keep her privacy with me, close to my heart for as long as I can. My silence is a sacrifice to the lasting love I still feel for her.

When she left me Salvador's pain returned and I felt the need to prove myself once more. Not to me but to the people I knew before and those that had consigned me to a footnote in our circle of the arts.

The week I decided to sell paintings again I went up to London to see Salvador's gallery. It had been open for fifteen years but I hadn't gone there as I knew I would be seen and then people would talk of me again. I wanted to be invisible. I finally went there and walked through and stopped at each painting and saw the truth in ever greater light. Salvador's early work was bold and passionate and arresting. He used vibrant colours and sharp lines to bring peoples focus towards what he wanted them to see, I used the same technique for my Nebula, the one David loved.

The painting I love most in Salvador's gallery in London is the one of the old woman, a life time of feelings and emotions etched across her face, her eyes deep with wisdom, her skin marked by her time on the Homeworld while she stands in a society of perpetual youth. I adore it so much and I could afford it but I won't purchase it. It hangs there to remind the world of what someone is capable of under extreme conditions. It reminds me of how good I am at what I do and it will always remind Salvador not of what he took from me but of what I took from him.

Looking through the collection I could see where he had lost his way. His art had become expensive and he was seen as the very best and so he no longer had anything to prove, or maybe he became tired or addicted to drink and social movements? It was probably a combination of all of those things. Either way there was a clear point when I could see he had started inviting apprentices and terrorising them and stealing their work. Walking round I realised he had been doing it for far longer than I had thought possible, at least twenty years prior to his encounter with me.

He is still a celebrated artist but they say his work became stale after his time with me and that he never painted the same after I left. Was I his muse? They loved to ask him and he says nothing but I see the truth in his eyes each time he is asked. No, I am not his muse. I am the woman that broke him.

He paints still, using just what he feels now and sells it for large sums of currency while his old apprentices are all said to be 'too much like their old master' to give real credence to. They learnt to copy his greatness, not to become great themselves.

Do the critics really know the truth? Do they care? I don't know the answer but I do know I stopped him from victimising people and stealing their work. I know I broke his will and showed him that I was an artist and then proved it by going away and not coming back until the world had almost forgotten about my time with him and I know that when I returned they said I was a true talent of global appeal.

You see I paint differently now to how I had with him those months and in my life before Salvador Iranie. I had learnt to distance myself from him and I have surpassed him, not because I have more money and power than he has, that is not the case at all, no; I am an artist and always will be, with a love for what I do so strong that it can carry me over any mountain. He is diminished while I have risen from the ashes and I look back and wonder if I should feel sorry for him but I can't.... He was a bastard.

CHAPTER NINETEEN

DECK FOURTEEN

I had trained myself to never think about Salvador, spent years directing my attentions elsewhere to not relive those days but I found that sitting with his portrait brought clarity. The experience had been an incredibly hard one but I had survived and in my own way I had triumphed. There were many nights that I brought him out on his own and watched him, remembering his cruelty. I would actively remember the fear of those assaults and the humiliation in my defeat, yet I found that with each session I had with Salvador I felt lighter, less hampered by his negative impact on my life. Finally I allowed myself one last luxury and as I sat with him I allowed myself to cry. I cried remembering his house and then I found myself laughing; Laughing because it was through his homes technology that I was now realising my dreams. I thought of Salvador and I realised I did not need to hurt him anymore, I did not need to entertain him, or cower at his name. I took him out and walked him down to deck fourteen and placed him in storage. I didn't hide him. He was not banished. He simply wasn't important anymore.

With Salvador gone my mind felt free and my spirits actually lifted. I ran harder and became fitter, studied plants and colours from the new world and addressed the question that plagued me for a week until finally I discovered the thing that I needed; a breakthrough that would see me engage in artistic activity a new: I found I had no idea how to paint the new flora, to capture the raised textures of the leaves and the more outrageous colours and so needed to teach myself. Deck fourteen became a study space; a flowing experiment into whether or not I could master what I was about to be surrounded by and as the days started to turn over on each other I found the work more and more absorbing.

The new planet was abundant in life and though it was similar to Homeworld the light was different due to the dual sons, with darkness only coming for a few hours each day. Forty percent of the globe was covered in land with the three continents taking only fifty five percent of that land, the other forty five percent was made up of hundreds of thousands of small islands, all teeming with flora.

The petals and leaves on these plants were huge and twice as thick as their equivalents on Homeworld. They were nearly always concaved with serrated edges and the scent of the flowers was expected to be of a far higher concentration than we were used to. The veins running across the palms of the leaves were a deeper colour than that of the leaf itself making the sap look like rich blood being pumped around an active system, far more human-like than in any plant I had ever seen and the colours were so much more vibrant. Capturing this accurately without being able to touch it was almost impossible and yet I believed I could indeed succeed.

The Graphene walls could respond to current in a number of amazing ways, one of these was that the walls could change texture. Salvador's mansion had been programmed with multiple settings and I had learned to operate the system while there at that accursed place, to change the currents and program the walls to do as he had wished. I took those skills and I spent a whole month programming the plants that I wanted, from both Homeworld and our new home. As you entered deck fourteen you would see the new world with its Kaleidoscope of colour etched into the walls, slowly as you walked down the twisting corridor the plants would change into the familiar flowers of Homeworld until you came to rest in the large room at the end. I would study the new and flow through to the old until I understood the relationship between the two. By the end of the project I would understand this journey not by looking forwards, but by looking back.

The new world would be alien to me until I understood its relationship to the old. I didn't consciously chose this way of working, could not have reasoned this project into existence. I 'felt' this process as I worked, programming plants and downloading structures for the walls to imitate. The white, lifeless, jutting out pieces of wall would only differ by a maximum of twelve millimetres and yet when I pressed the initiate button I was amazed at the results. Without colour and under the standard light that illuminated the corridor it was like watching the most complicated wallpaper ripple into life, but I knew I could make this into something truly befuddling. I could fool myself and others with my complicated illusion and perhaps, I wondered, was this why I was here? Why the colonial council selected me in the first place?

I was contemplating this as I ran through the decks when I stumbled and fell awkwardly. I shifted on the floor and tried to stagger up and continue straight on but pain shot through my leg and forced me back to the deck. I lay on the floor covered in sweat for a minute before I regained control and shifted to a sitting position. Opposite me through the large clear glass viewing portals were rows and rows of colonists slumbering. I looked into the centre of that cluster and saw my muse.

I struggled to my feet and limped forward, aware of a large cut on my left leg. I rested on the glass and watched her sleeping, unaware of me and my focus upon her. What was she dreaming of? Would she remember me standing here when she awakened? Would she know what she meant to me or how many hours I'd stood on this spot staring at her, imagined her waking and coming to me in my quarters late at night and copulating with me as Lucile and Gareth had; passion and urgency flowing from every pour?

I reached down to my leg and felt the blood covering my lower leg, gathering some onto my fingertips I started to smear it on the window, at first in small, self conscious dabs but as a picture formed in my head I started to work faster, more frantically, painting a heart onto the clear graphene. My fingers dug at the cut to bring more blood from the wound and as it flowed I filled in the heart and wrote 'I LOVE YOU' backwards so that she would read it as soon as she opened her eyes.

I limped backwards and looked at the window. Staring at the crudely fashioned heart; I realised what I was doing was not only unhygienic but it was also unacceptable. I looked up and down the corridor in case someone saw me and then pulled off my top. I lunged forward and started rubbing the window with my running shirt, desperately trying to remove the smeared blood and ended up banging on the window screaming 'WAKE UP! WAKE UP! PLEASE FUCKING WAKE UP!'

I blew myself out after a few minutes and slumped back down to the floor. I wondered what Idris would think of me now? Shivering with fear and confusion, half naked outside the cryo-bays, blood smeared and crazy and looking every inch like the terrifying reincarnation of Quartermaster Williams. I sobbed and then looked up at the camera, aware that the Buckingham was watching everything I did and making judgements on my continued sanity.

I sat down and forced myself to check my leg, the cut was deep but it wasn't a big deal at all, even after I'd forced it to weep more crimson for my horrifying painting it was just a flesh wound and easily sealed. It was now that I needed someone like Idris far more than I did my muse; someone dependable and safe and soothing, someone to help me keep myself from losing this terrible battle against loneliness and despair.

I remembered the twenty representatives of the colonial council sitting before me on white marble steps, like representatives of the Roman Empire, food and drink enough for all as they conducted my interview. It did not worry me to be in front of them but I knew that I was perhaps not the most emotive of people and so was concerned that I would not come across as the right candidate on an interview of this kind.

This concern was addressed by their leader, Idris Felon, a dark skinned man with a square jaw and a warrior's build. He was powerful instead of toned and direct in his action and focus. If he was looking at you it was hard not to know. If he liked you it was obvious, if he didn't it was equally as clear.

He pointed to the centre and asked me to begin my interview by capturing their images. I had prepared the materials and had them stored at the back of the hall and so stepped forward and removed the large canvas they had placed in the centre of the room. I had no intention of painting them as decadent senators or of using paint at all for that matter, instead I rolled out clear sheets of paper thin Graphene, set them to become rigid and then ran a charge thought them to lock them together.

From the steps came muttering and hushed conversation, I wondered if they were discussing what I was doing but felt that focusing on their reaction would not help me artistically and so I blocked out their noise and moved the materials I needed forward. All told there were twelve five kilogram bags, each one with a different coloured fine, dry sand inside. I started to cast the sand around to build a picture of the colonists on the floor, like a reflection of themselves in a pool of marble.

I had read their brief and had noticed that they were keen on the new, not the fashionable, but the genuinely new. I looked into state of the art methods of colour spraying and design but nothing struck me as being of significant depth to bring the result I desired from them, which was complete conviction in my ability to perform the task ahead. The room was semi circular and the steps stretched right around the curve of the room, bright summer sunshine blazed through the clear glass ceiling touching them with golden light.

I observed them as they sat and talked about the colony amongst themselves and asked me questions. Many were about my famous father (a legend in the planning of off world colonies and a major contributor to this one in terms of finance and planning) and mother (a woman many came to know as the 'scarlet woman of the Union of Briton). I answered without malice about my mother and had certainly learned to control what I felt towards her, for my father I did the same. In time they brought up Salvador and I kept my answers short for they were not there to learn about his lack of talent but of my abundance in it.

    I made an image of them on the Graphene floor canvas, accessed the canvas's controls and then beckoned them down to view it. They had all seen the evolution of this accurate and pleasing image of themselves in sand and were keen to look closer, but when I told them to touch it, to step into it, to explore and alter it some of them became confused. Why would I want them to destroy what I had taken time and care to make?

    I sat down and had a drink and invited them to do so even though the image would be altered and some of them did indeed put a line where their clothes gathered or pushed sand until it seemed they were poking the person next to them. They would step back and laugh and look at me to see if I was angry and I would encourage them to interact further with what I had crafted for them.

    Idris sat down beside me on the highest step and smiled as he put his arm around me. He was a huge man and I became aware of how much he dwarfed me when we were in close contact.

'I can see people interacting and enjoying what you have given us, but it is not permanent,' he said in his deep voice. I looked into his young face and caught his bright eyes, eyes they were surrounded by small scars earned in combat. He was proud of his past and accomplishments in the ring as a participant in blood sports but I have never seen the point in them myself.

'The panels are locked together by an electric charge. The sand has been treated and mixed with tiny metal fragments. When I was finished I recorded the exact positions of each grain of sand on the sheets. When I feed the right frequency through the sheeting the sand will shift to those positions exactly and it is currently recording the image on the floor every thirty seconds,' I replied pointing at the plugged in tablet situated to the side of the image on the floor. 'You can have a permanent record and piece of art that can be hung from any wall, yet it is also easy to move and disassemble. It is only as temporary as you wish it to be.' Idris laughed and squeezed me tighter. In truth I think he looked impressed.

'But what truly is Permanent? Even legends slip away in time.' I looked down at a young man staring at his rough, sand rendered face and I saw him smile, but it was a smile touched with sadness. I knew he was Idris's partner and so looked to Idris for understanding. As we looked down the man etched lines down his face; the face changed from a smooth and youthful rogues into that of an old man's who had seen so many things.

'I know you are married, but how is it that you stay close when there is so long a time to be together? Do you not worry that he will change or you will?' I asked the colony leader and he became serious, I was aware that what he was going to tell me something that meant a great deal to him. Something that was real to him.

'The illusion is that we stay the same,' he said as he pointed down at the sand now being more and more widespread as others moved in to see for themselves. 'The fact is we are always changing. We become closer and then more distant; like the moon our feelings wax and wane, but the moon is constant as well. Just because you cannot see it does not mean it isn't there. ' He twisted his wedding ring; a simple white gold band, around his finger as he spoke. His connection with the ring seemed so strong that simply wearing it wasn't enough. He had to feel it, touch it, as though it were always in his thoughts.

'It is what it is and that is never perfect... But I can say that we have respect for each other, love that ebbs and flows like the ocean but like the ocean always there are waves. The love never leaves and we understand that to be as we are now we must accept that we were different when we first met, and will be different in another fifty years.'

'Fifty years? I know it's not uncommon but still, how long will it continue? How do you know you will be together that long and how can you be prepared for the pain if it ends?' Estoban; Idris's partner, looked up at us and was nodding his approval as he drew a smile across the old man's face with his finger. Idris squeezed me tighter than he had been before and looked at me deeply.

'I do not prepare for a parting and I always hope for the best for our union. I work hard to bring him happiness and he does the same for me. He also thinks your fantastic and I happen to agree.'

'Fantastic enough to get a place on your colony as your artist?' I asked with my eyebrows raised.

'Fantastic enough to come with us and be loved for whom you are and not who you were or what you represented,' he answered smiling wickedly as though the excitement of what was to come had gripped him suddenly. It was an infectious smile and though I was normally biologically immune to that sort of socially passed expression I found myself smiling back.

'We want to bring this expedition to life, not just document it but make it live and breathe. We are moving to a place that is so abundant in beauty that an image taken from a lens just isn't enough. We want you to show people the colour and the paradise that we have found and we are to send back cloth with the amazing dyes we know we can produce, but we also want our world to be known for its arts. Its music, its dance, and its art; we want to build a new artistic identity, we want its colour to be vibrant, it's perspective one of hope and amazement at the blessings the universe has bestowed upon us and joy that we have had the courage to pursue those blessings. We want to have someone that will bring us a style that will be like nothing else in the universe... I think you can do that. Do you?'

'Yes.'

'Then you are the artist we are looking for,' he answered and hugged me triumphantly.

'Idris, if I am to have this position and responsibility then my conditions must be met before I can join your colony.' I spoke seriously and he reciprocated.

'We will meet them all,' was all he answered and he was true to his word.

*

I looked at the walls with their three dimensional effect that conveyed the exact nature of each of the plants textures and initiated the ceiling pattern. A light, colourless canopy sprang to life, with breaks for golden light to seep through in strong shafts. Looking at the first small section of my twisting corridor I realised I could not wait to get started and was about to prepare my first brushes when a soft echoing alarm drifted into the corridor.

At first I was completely confounded as to why I was not hungry, that was the dinner bell I had programmed after all. Then it dawned on me that this was not a time to eat but in fact an alarm to warn me of a serious fault in The Buckingham's systems.

I raced to the bridge with my heart pounding as I knew anything that went wrong now was serious due to the drifting nature of the ship. Only so many systems were operational in the ships dormant mode and so there would be repercussions from what I found in that room. That conclusion was inescapable.

I took up my place in the captain's chair and locked my P.S.M.P into the main computer. I watched the ships schematic burst onto the wall in front of me and immediately knew that this would make my stay even more difficult but I never wavered in my conviction to make sure the ship was my main priority.

The blue line of damage report flowed through the engine room and into the life support section. I could see a choice was clear and so I took it. If I didn't act very quickly then a section of the cryogenic compartments would fail and a substantial number of colonists would awaken. In these conditions it was obvious that twenty thousand people would not be able to remain alive on board for a long time in restricted quarters so I cut off life support to the rest of the ship, rerouted the power to the cryogenic compartments and sealed myself into the small section of ship that constituted deck fourteen through to eight. I managed to reroute power so that I could keep the kitchen running and the heating operational and then consigned the rest of the ship over to power saving. I watched the section seals lock and felt my living space deplete by ninety eight percent.

All of my runs, all of my climbs and all of the cryogenic compartments were now completely cut off from me. Med bay, the observation deck, storage and all the human faces I'd become used to running past were all gone at the touch of a button. I watched the power reallocate and it was confirmed that no systems were now in danger. I had saved them. The final system to lose power was the long range and short range sensors. Now I would not know if a rescue ship was outside the door or two months away. I was blind.

This hadn't bothered me too much until now, it was something that I had no control over and so was not worth wasting energy on and yet now I looked at the dead console my heart sank. Would I be here forever? No, because as much as I knew I could take the isolation better than anyone else on the custodial crew even I knew I had limitations. Starved of stimulus it was only a matter of time before I would suffer isolation sickness. It was almost funny, but it really wasn't, because I knew I wouldn't be able to hold out forever and the thought of a delayed rescue ship finding me wandering the same limited corridors, deranged by my ordeal made my stomach tighten till it hurt.

CHAPTER TWENTY

BLESSED

Ivan sat opposite me in silence and watched me eat. He was quite handsome really, when you looked at him without the sneer and the dirt and the chip on his shoulder that gave him a slightly slanted look to his stance.

His face was symmetrical and he had some depth to those features and even greater to those eyes. Yet he seemed to still be my enemy. Salvador had been vanquished and the others gathered were lovers, friends and family (I didn't think you could classify family as the enemy; at least not to anyone outside the family). Ivan stood out like a sore thumb.

Why had I taken him as a subject? What relevance did he have to this trip bar the minor irritation of knowing that someone in the room resents you for reasons that you could never effect; having a view you could seemingly never alter?

I had painted him as I had observed him on the ship; muscular and mucky, intelligent but closed minded. I would not go so far as to say that he lacked character or soul but certainly he was more straight forward in his approach to life than me and cared little for the arts. What good were they to him anyway? He was a man of science and though many people could live with the two in their lives he clearly couldn't.

As I watched him I was struck by how little I knew about him. I was always of the opinion that if someone didn't want to talk to you the worst thing you could do was inject yourself into their personal space. Surely that was exactly what they did not want you to do and so by definition would be massively counterproductive to that relationship. He had never shown that much interest, perhaps even I would go so far as to say he had gone out of his way to show disinterest in my presence.

Now he sat opposite me, my only guest at the breakfast table. What was he doing here? I swallowed down some orange juice and knowing that I had nearly an hour before I needed to be anywhere I decided to converse with Ivan; to try to remove the thorn that I had obviously placed in his paw.

'Ivan, have I offended you in some way?' He replied with the normal level of conversation he had delivered since leaving the Buckingham on the repair run.

'If it's something I've done then I do wish you'd just say it, the silent treatment is getting boring.'

Nothing. Okay, this was obviously going to have to be a Q&A session driven by me.

'I think back and find nothing that I have said or done that would offend you prior to the final supper we shared and so it can't be something I have said or done, but instead some principal that you feel I have betrayed.' Was that the hint of recognition crossing that face? Had I started down the right road finally?

'You dislike my status as Princess of the Union of Briton? That much is true but I think what's important is why you dislike that title so much. What does it represent to you?' He seemed to shift in his place (of course he didn't really, but my mind worked better to imagine these movements; these reactions. I wasn't mad, I just needed to pretend that I wasn't just talking to paint and canvas or face the fact I was chatting to inanimate objects).

'Are you jealous? Why would anyone be jealous of me? I did not have an easy upbringing,' my statement was factual but then who could say that their childhood was completely full of light anyway? There cannot be light without darkness, waiting to steal in and smother our hope and expose our fears.

'No. No, you were not jealous... You were, and still are, resentful. Thinking back to that brief inappropriate laugh we had together while Lucile and Gareth stood frozen, it became very awkward for you very quickly, not so much because you felt bad for Lucile and Gareth but because... Because you felt guilty for laughing with me.' I frowned. What was wrong with seeking and making emotional or social connections with me? What about me made him feel uncomfortable?

'I have to tell you Ivan that I'm not happy that you'd think it wrong to speak to me. Why? What is wrong with knowing me?!' It was clear that I was becoming far more irritated than he was. I had had this sort of thing happen before in the dining room and could see this was going to become too personal, too quickly, for my liking, and so decided to finish up.

'Ivan, I'm going to see to my duties and deck fourteen and then we'll pick this up at dinner, when we can be more civil.' I stood and carried my plate and glass into the kitchen leaving him alone to contemplate how best to broach the subject tonight.

*

I completed my checks and spent the rest of the day in deck fourteen, the meticulous task of capturing the colour of moonstruck petals from a planet I had never even set foot on was maddening until I finally felt that I had got it right, and even then I couldn't bring myself to fully believe I had captured their essence yet, I'd need to see the plants first hand before I could truly congratulate myself.

Inserting sections of night to contrast the day proved incredibly difficult but also incredibly rewarding when I came to view the result it had upon me as I walked through the different sections. It was simply amazing.

The time in the garden on deck fourteen drew most of my energy from me and so I arrived at the dinner table after freshening up clouded by exhaustion. I looked up from my plate and there he sat... Waiting for me. I was later than usual and knew it would be unacceptable to continue without apologising.

'I'm sorry I'm late Ivan, I had rather more to do than I had considered earlier and you know how I hate slips in punctuality. It's just rude, so I'm sorry.'

Ivan didn't move, it was as though he'd been there all day just considering the conversation we were about to embark on.

'Fine, so you're going to be offended, I can understand that.'

Ivan was still and I suppose many would akin our exchange as about as interesting as watching paint dry, which is something that has always captured me in fact. Watching your paint change shades slightly as it dries is fascinating ,or when it's struck by the light; the texture altering and becoming what you thought it would be or, on rare occasions, when it does something unexpected and looks differently to how you thought it would. Those times only come when I'm experimenting now but as a child watching my paint dry was in fact an exhilarating experience. So I would say it was far less interesting than that.

I ate and felt my strength grow by the mouthful. I was aware he was there and he was aware that I had decided to make him wait; I had decided to be rude as he had been rude to me. I drank, swallowed and loved each fork full before I pushed my plate away and then to add insult to injury I went to wash up. It took a mere five minutes and yet in that time I came upon a sharp discovery.

My hands plunged into the water of the sink and I recoiled my left in pain. Holding my hand up I had cut my index finger on the chopping knife; a knife I normally washed separately to make sure this sort of thing didn't happen. Blood ran from the tip of my finger and I could see that the incision wasn't deep and yet it hurt a great deal.

I stood by the sink, squeezing the tip of my finger and staring at the blood as it snaked down my palm and to my wrist. I watched it until suddenly I became afraid of the blood as it slipped down my forearm, remembering the blood heart on the window and the moment of slipped reality. I grabbed a towel and covered the wound, then quickly wiped the blood off of my skin. I looked at the smeared blood and realised that my skin had lightened since I had come aboard, not by a great deal but by enough for me to notice. That rich chocolate colour that many of my lovers had expressed a great love for was paler and though there was nothing wrong with any colour of skin it did look wrong on me. I made sure all the blood was off, cleaned the wound and sprayed seal skin over the top of my finger, then returned to the dinner table with a glass of water.

Ivan was still. I was sitting, considering my skin and the throb of my finger when I looked up at his impassive face; he was watching me, Like he had always done.

This was not a face of love or attraction; it was something else, something far more familiar. He was studying me.

I sat exposed and recognised the impassive eyes of judgement and realised they were my own. I walked forward and looked into his face and to my shock I looked into my own eyes. I had quite literally painted Ivan with my eyes! Why? And how could I not have noticed until now?

I sat close and studied him as he studied me and then sat back. He was a mirror as I was for him. We saw each other, yet we also saw ourselves.

I looked back and thought about how I acted around him and it was certainly true that I was guarded, mainly because I thought he was judging me constantly, perhaps that's how he viewed me? Did he see me as being like him or did he see me as being cold and uninterested in him? Was that how I appeared to other people? Was my reaction to Ivan how other people reacted to me?

Ivan had always appeared cold, unfriendly and ingenuous to me. He was a man of privilege seeking tasks of a physical nature to compensate for his affluence. He was a man of high education, skill and intelligence that deadened his off time with practical mechanics and engine repairs. He would do what others were not prepared too to make himself fit in... To apologise for his self-perceived superiority.

I felt slightly sick. Was this how others saw me? Was this what I was even doing? Cleaning up after others because I was a princess and I felt the need to prove I was no better than everyone else, yet so in doing appeared to make myself stand apart? Even worse was the idea that I did in fact see myself as being superior. Did I? Was I better than everyone else?!

As I looked at Ivan I realised that perception and reality were slightly different. If others saw me as purposefully under achieving so that I could fit in then they had got it all wrong. I was an artist and one of the very best, I hadn't under achieved, I'd excelled. I took this job as custodial crew maintenance officer to make sure I had the time to paint while on voyage and knew I would need a distraction from the painting and refused to just sit around. What I was doing was not apologetically serving! I was being useful!

So what of Ivan? What was his story?! He was incapable of telling me and yet he had decided to show me how others perceived me, so I would turn my eye to him with a generosity I hadn't afforded him before.

He was a smart kid from a rich family who had shown him the value of hard work. He learnt and was driven to seek a goal and achieved that with application and hard work. He was a doctor with several specialisations and commanded a very handsome wage for his efforts and yet what he did now did not require a vast amount of his time. As an expert he was needed but in reality his skills were only really needed when everything was going wrong and that was not common on colonial ships as each stage is planned meticulously. Even for his six months on the colony he was unlikely to be needed for anything more than adjustment therapy and standard medical doctor work.

He learned early in his life that a self imposed distraction could be a very useful tool and so had become very interested in mechanical engineering and.... No, he had taught himself about the old combustion engines and worked his way up from there, the dirtier the work the better as it proved to be so different from his cryogenic specialties. He does it to keep himself active, use the muscle he trains for and so justifies the time it takes to hone his body everyday and because; above all else and most simply; it interests him.

He is driven, intelligent and knowledgeable but that is not who he is, that is simply what he's like. Those are skills and traits and though they do effect how he acts, what he says, and what he does, but they do not define him completely... He has a personality. One that is strong enough to allow him to follow his interests without fear of what others will say and yet... He knows he is privileged.

Perhaps the fault was mine.

I watched him and then went to leave. I wanted to go but stopped at the door and forced myself to come back to the other end of the table. I had something I needed to say, something I didn't want to and yet needed to, perhaps I was even brave enough to admit to myself that it was something I had not been aware of before and so it was going to sound like an apology.

I stood before him but addressed everyone in the room against the walls and Lucile in the kitchen, I even imagined that my voice pierced the walls and could be heard by Salvador.

'I do not clean up after people because Salvador made me do it or because I am trying to prove I don't have a superiority complex. I do it because I find it soothing and I like the idea of being helpful to others.'

That went well and I nearly left on that note but then I found myself clearing my throat and addressing the collective once more.

'I know I feel that my upbringing was not one that showed me an excess of love or compassion… But I do see that it afforded me many things that I would not have had if my father and mother were not who they were.'

Silence. A stunned silence, I thought, as I felt more and more exposed.

'I can be hard to live with and I guard my feelings. I do not make connections easily and can appear cold. I feel as you do, just not as intensely and… And I'm sorry if you feel I hold you in disregard. I want to be able to make connections, I want to be able to be friends and I want to be more open.'

No comment from the gathered paintings, just a deathly silence that lingered once my words were gone.

'All I can do is try.'

I looked at them all and left the room with my head held low. I didn't feel weak or cheap but instead sad; saddened by the thought of all those people coming into my life only to be met by the impassable wall of my emotional barriers and the terrible perception of superiority that it created around me.

CHAPTER TWENTY ONE

WHEN THE RAIN COMES

I would tell you of the day to day existence but that is already recorded, there for all to see. I don't think it's important how many times a walked the corridors a day or how much I ate suffice to say I stayed alive. Of course it was in the plan that I would have to be prepared to face an outcome of this kind; a delayed rescue vessel leading me to prolonged isolation.

I knew I would suffer from such things as sensory deprivation and so took to sleeping with both dolls and synchronized their breathing so I could have a full night with two warm bodies and for a time that was enough. I continued to do all the things David and I had discussed that would be important to my survival, proper nutrition, routine, masturbation and sanitation. I had however hit the point where silence itself was an enemy and even though I had never really listened to music before (I was never interested in it as I found it just drowned out my own thoughts) I found myself hungering for something to replace the soft humming of the ship.

At first it was a basis of trial and error, like a child trying to explore colours in a pallet I mixed and dipped and dabbed. Some reggae, some jazz, some Martian synth thrash, easy listening, progressive rock, space opera, funk, Titan swing, big band, minimalistic one piece, orchestral, Bhangra, Blues, synth, pop, Homeworld traditional, colonial metal, French union new electro... The list was endless and the sounds so varied that I was convinced several times that I wouldn't find something that helped, and yet I did. It took weeks of cycling through the memory banks and sampling each style before I realised I preferred peaceful and reflective music only to also come into contact with 'new-techno' or 'rapid' as it's widely called; a synthetically created sound using drum machines that fired at inhuman speeds, but the base would hammer along with my heart as I ran. A question I struck upon was this: wasn't all music 'synthetic'? Objects and materials manipulated to bring different sounds and pitches in an effort to induce different moods in the listener and provoke different reactions.

Running was now confined to key areas due to the lockdown so I had lost all of my challenging courses and was now forced to do laps of the corridor up and down. It was dull and so I found myself pushing into the realms of shuttle running and found the punishing routine drew more sweat from me than ever before. I began to really enjoy this new mix of intense physical exercise and thundering noise, it drowned out the silence that would have filled that space till all the air had been driven out and there was only me left, suffocating in loneliness and depression.

I am not one to complain and I have no real need for circumstantial contact with other people, but that was exactly what I needed. The panther returned in my dreams and I would welcome her with loving arms compared to the horror of my other nightmares. I would fall asleep and then wake up and find that the doors had been made transparent. Entering the corridors I would walk along to where the cryogenic bays were and instead of cold Graphene in front of me I would peer through the transparent aperture to see people walking around, preparing for the landing on our new colony. I would wave and cheer until I realised that I had been left here on purpose, that they were never going to let me out and I was doomed to live alone until I died of my isolation.

Other nights I would dream that I was still asleep and that the colonists were wandering the halls outside my door like ghosts, pale and still in a stasis sleep yet able to walk and pace and stand and stare. I would wake and walk out to find them there in the dining room, all standing behind paintings with knives and as I walked in they would slash my only friends to pieces leaving them tattered and dead on the floor. I would wake crying and as much as I could not be a good judge of my own mental condition I was aware that I would become a danger to myself if I didn't find a way to handle the isolation. Yet I could find no way out.

   I dreamed of waking the colonists at random and copulating with them, a ghostly Chad Williams jeering us on in our lustful fits. On other occasions I would open an unthreatening door and as I stepped into the room I would realise it was the Core Control room. Before I could avert my eyes Leon and my father would drop from the ceiling with nooses around their necks and thrash around in front of me as I watched, unable to move to help them till their feet stopped twitching. Finally I would rush forward and try to take my father's weight and save him but when I did he would laugh at me and I would wake screaming.

   There was no way out and yet no way to live inside, yet that too is an exaggeration of the situation. Deck fourteen was a place that consumed me completely, when there I was not alone on a ship of just under five hundred thousand sleeping adventurers, I was in a jungle of colour and texture of my own invention. I would look at those petals rising out from the wall and I would smile and touch them and feel the ridges and paint them as delicately as I could. In there it all had to be perfect and it was. My night and day sections made painting the flowers so complicated I would suffer strong headaches that made me feel sick after working on the deck. Capturing the look that the real plants had under the three moons and in the twin suns was as difficult as I had imagined and then more so.

   All was fine when in the confines of that deck but I also knew I needed to make sure I had time away from that place so that my obsession did not lead to mistakes or an increase in my condition when out of that long snaking corridor.

   I would open the door to leave the work and would be thrown into turmoil as I looked into the corridor, knowing that the dreams and empty, soulless spaces were all that waited for me.

*

It was cold when I woke the morning change came, cold in the room and cold under the blankets. I felt the chill and knew today would be a day of decision, of action, so I waited for a few minutes under the covers, shivering yet unwilling to confront the reality that surrounded me; power was failing.

Finally I simply couldn't take the cold anymore and had to get out of bed. I looked around to see the air fog with my breath and the strange bleached colour of the walls and floor, the temperature effecting their surfaces, covering them in particles of frost.

I pulled the blanket around me and made my way to the main bridge with my P.S.M.P. Looking at it confirmed that I was in dire need of fixing power couplings but the true nature of my position became clear when the 'action required' screen gave me clear directions to the 'Power Coupling Re-initialiser (external)'.

I read it and re-read it before it sank in fully and normally I would have just accepted its ruling and prepared for the appropriate action but something made me stop and hold my breath. I had come to find the empty space of the corridors as desolate and crushingly saddening, how would I be able to take the vastness of space that surrounded 'The Buckingham'? That was even if I could get out there.

Once sealed into the section I had thought there was no way out until power could be restored, but now this fault occurring had opened up a new line of attack. If I had to go outside what if I could make other repairs? What if I could bring back power to other sections of the ship? Free myself from the prison I had been locked in and at least find some room to breathe? I could run freely through the ship again, see the colonists, paint things that captured my eye in distant corners of The Buckingham! I checked the schematics and linked them to the medical program, it was important to know how long I had before the loss of power to the environmental controls would kill me.

I consulted the technical advice concerning the repairs and was amazed to find that I knew exactly what I was doing. I had studied long and hard when young and with no deterioration in the memory cells in my brain at all I could recall with striking accuracy the lessons that I sat through right up to my sixteenth birthday. Of, course I had read since then and kept up with modern trends and new breakthroughs in technology but I had assumed that this was going to be difficult and it really wasn't. All I needed to do was change from the primary electrical net that ran round the ship to the secondary; it meant punching in a code and flicking a switch. The problem was that the internal control ports were fried due to Gareth and Lucile's escapades so I would have to go to the external ports.

I wanted to know why the port was external and I wanted to grab the person that designed the system and strangle them until I looked it up and it turned out to be my father. I stopped and shivered and checked the medical action statement.

If I accessed the emergency sealed systems suit located on the bridge I could last for a week if I tapped into the air supply. I looked at the schematic and found the compartment for the suit concealed at the back of the room. How the hell had I not known it was there?! Was I blind?! I set off for the suit quickly as I could feel the cold intensifying and knew I would have to hurry if I wanted to make sure I was still sensible enough to get the job done.

The bridge was as cold as the rest of the corridors and it took me several seconds before I could see the almost seamless cupboard at the back of the room. I went to it and opened the door, feeling the cold pulling at my limbs and making my teeth chatter involuntarily. The suit was slim but loose and in one neat, well tailored piece. I pulled it on and felt its soft material against my skin, smooth and light yet, incredibly strong. Wasting no time I pulled the large, knee high boots over my feet and the internal sensors expanded the Archimedes foam on the inside so that they fitted perfectly. I held the helmet in my hands and explored it with my fingers, unsure of why I was so resistant to putting it on yet knowing it was inevitable. I took my final breath of chilled air and then pulled the helmet over my head.

The glass dome had a clearance of roughly two inches away from my face and as I twisted it and locked the seal onto the neckpiece my breath steamed the front of the Graphene glass. I switched on the power and instantly the suit began to heat to room temperature, in two minutes I was warm and surprisingly comfortable. I didn't like the helmet and so I buried that dislike at the back of my head as I would a personal dislike for another person while talking to them so as not to appear rude.

I called up all the relevant data on the bridges screen and then waited for a plan to form, when the computer gave me the option of the simplest of repairs I logged the information in a folder and accessed the level three and above repair jobs.

The first required a large amount of materials that were not on the ship and was designed to bring the whole system back on line. I knew this wasn't possible without the rescue ship and so I checked the second option and it required rerouting the power on several points on the outer hull. This would effect the flow of power from the secondary generator and so would bring the secondary grid online. I would have full run of the ship again. I sat and wondered what I would do if let out of my cage again and felt excitement and desire rush through my system. It would be glorious but would it also be dangerous?

Looking at the detailed plans and repair guides I could see they would be easy and straight forward to perform and yet that was only half the story. I would have to leave the ship and spend at least half a day wandering across the outer hull, a practice still deemed very dangerous and certainly not to be done alone... And yet that was the only way I could do it.

I checked the details and realised I would need to be outside for at least twelve hours, a dream to many and yet the reality of the swallowing blackness of space terrified me. What if it became too much? To perform the repairs I would have to take what was left of the primary grid offline and that would mean no external lights and no power to the airlocks till I had completed my task. There was no danger of the suit becoming damaged or air running our really, I could be hooked into the supply from an external port located by every external station and the suit could withstand incredible impacts. The problem was the disorientation of being outside in the pitch black. The Buckingham was huge and a wrong turn in the dark out there could see me easily becoming lost as the hull was covered in material pods that were attached to the main hull using magnetic prongs, ready to be detached on arrival.

I could hook my P.S.M.P into the ships navigator and save myself from that eventuality but still the environment would be hostile. I could use the magnetic boots but if I did that it would take me twice as long to navigate the ship, if I went for a tether rope I would have to deal with the idea that I may float off if I made a mistake while switching my tether cord from grid to grid. It was dangerous.

I was brought back to a simple question; why would anyone make it so difficult to switch to the secondary power relay? What good did it do the ship or either its custodian or colonial set up crews? I was drawn back to the designer of the system, a pioneer in the world of colonial ship organisation and structural administration. He was a man that people respected for his professional wisdom and well thought out plans. His experience in colonial matters was almost second to none and yet this struck me as being incredibly stupid; almost worthy of calling him an imbecile.

Why and how he had decided the backup secondary relay switch should be situated on the external hull of the ship, it was surely madness? Perhaps he had come up with so many practical and helpful suggestions over the years that he was due one that defied sense and logic? I checked the computer for a status reading on my suit and it confirmed all seals were locked properly and that I was now fully protected from the elements that surrounded me. Obviously it was now not a question of if I would go outside but when and then the question would be for what reason? To reset the overall secondary power relay; so unlocking the ship, or would I play it safe and just reset the backup system and power up my several deck wide prison that felt tiny compared to the rest of the ship?

I didn't want to go back to what I had started to refer to as 'The Stockade' and so decided pretty much on the spot that I would switch off the main grid and spend the time outside. The thought of opening the airlock intimidated me already and yet there was no alternative. No way out (pun intended).

I needed to know why this was going to happen and so as I had all the relevant data compiled into my P.S.M.P I checked the system protocol and guided my way through the technical data written by an engineer to the notes from my father. I sat reading them as a bar on my P.S.M.P filled slowly with all the relevant information and also recharged it so that I would not lose power at a critical moment 'outside'.

'The backup secondary relay system is located on the external of the ship so as to make it difficult to access,' I sat reading my father's notes aloud to the room. 'This is necessary to dissuade any disgruntled or psychologically depleted member of the crew, either custodial or colonial, from interfering with the power relays and so damaging the vessel.' Was that all I was now? A 'psychologically depleted' member of the custodial crew? How the mighty had fallen.

'To shut down the system and reinitialise using the secondary relay should be a taxing task that would ideally require the skills and knowledge of three crew members yet it must also be a task that a singular crew member can achieve with the right focus and determination.' It made little sense to me but I continued presuming enlightenment was fast approaching.

'To this end the externalised secondary relay points will be positioned at great distance from each other on the hull, thus requiring a single crew member a great deal of travel time to reflect on the course of action being taken. If the repairs are necessary and the crew member capable (which all members should be) then the task is manageable but if the crew member is psychologically diminished or unfocused then the task will prove nearly impossible and so protect cryogenically frozen colonists from any repeat of the 'Williams event.' Here he had assumed the 'psychologically depleted would lack willpower, something not necessarily true.

'The computer will monitor the actions and habits of any single night-watchman and so safeguard the colonists from erratic or dangerous behaviour engaged in by the night-watchman (see figure 743 for details of 'evidence of erratic or deteriorating mental capacity' sub-routein). If the computer deems the night-watchman to be incapable then the sub-routine will instruct the life support systems to remove life sustaining capacity for a short time and then reboot the system. If the night-watchman becomes erratic or attempts to disrupt the computers designated objective then the computer will remove all command code clearance from the night-watchman removing their ability to open airlocks or pressure seals.'

I stopped reading and then read back again. Had the computer decided I was a threat to the colonists and contained me?! On my father's orders?! I walked away from the bridge apprehensive, not about the airlock now but the main door to my section, the one that I had sealed to save the colonists months earlier. Would that door open for me? If it didn't I would know that the days ahead would be my last, but if it opened then I would have a fighting chance.

There was no time to eat properly before leaving, though I did manage to slip the helmet off to eat an energy bar before reattaching it and heading for the door, aware that the coming ordeal would sap considerable energy.

I stood in the corridor and knew I would have to lock my bedroom door and the dining room to make sure they didn't completely freeze and so with that accomplished I went to the section pressure door and stood before it nervously. Punching in the door code was not difficult with the gloves I was wearing as they were quite tight and part of the body suit, but remembering the code was difficult as I was so convinced it was going to fail that I found it difficult to concentrate on the number sequence.

I inputted the code the computer had downloaded onto my P.S.M.P and I pressed the enter panel waiting for a rejection due to my 'diminished responsibility'. If that occurred I would face a trudge back to my bedroom to wait for death, yet thankfully that journey never came and I watched as the door unlocked magnetically and rumbled open. It was slower than normal due to the whole system conserving power. I looked out into the corridors beyond my section and smiled, the route I would take would bring me past my muse from deck eight and I would be able to watch her sleep one more time before I went out into the darkness, perhaps to say goodbye forever?

The boots were soft on the cold Graphene plastic floor as I walked through emergency lit corridors, approaching the cryogenic compartments with some anxiety. What would it mean to see her again? Would I weep? Was I as far gone as I thought I might be or was control still present in my system somewhere?

I turned and looked into the cryogenic compartment to see her placid face, relaxed in her slumber she looked even more beautiful than I remembered and yet it was not a sexual desire that crossed me, it was something far deeper. I felt almost paternally responsible for her now, her and her fellow colonists... My fellow colonists.

I watched for a while (perhaps longer than I should have) and then set off for the airlock. As I arrived I realised I wasn't carrying a tool belt at all and had to take a step back mentally to make sure I was going out there for the right reasons. I was going out to come back in, not simply to throw myself into space.

Having collected a tool kit that had the equipment needed and stashed it in a backpack designed for hull repair work I advanced on the airlock once more. The inner door opened smoothly and revealed the spare environmental suits, cords, safety lines and magnetic boots that were meant to be worn outside the ship. Having only done two short space walks before while training in orbit around Homeworld I was fairly sure that I was not qualified to make the decision as to which boots to wear and so consulted the safety protocols. They informed me that for long journeys on the ship's hull both a line and magnetic boots were advised.

'Upon placing your feet for works to be undertaken activate magnetic locking boots by depressing the magnetic activation button located on the boot tip. While traversing the hull use a long safety cord connected to the safety line runner,' I read and then dully placed the boot attachments over the ends of my existing enviro boots and attached a line to the inner wall of the airlock while I held a secondary line in my hand.

Stepping forward I activated the depressurisation protocol and waited for the air to be removed. I stayed motionless by that door for a few seconds looking out into the universe not with a sense of wonder but instead utter dread. It was black, all swallowing, and all consuming darkness. We were nowhere near a sun and so catching very little light at all. It would be worse when I exited because my first job would be to kill the power plunging me into the abyss.

Surely I should be able to see stars and Nebulas, constellations and planets; pin pricks of light in that sheet of oblivion? I could only surmise that I was suffering from a psychotic episode that had snuffed out the universe and was blocking my perception of their light. It seemed the logical explanation though not one I was happy to come too just before exiting The Buckingham.

The outer airlock opened easily and I floated out into the darkness, so thick it was like a solid barrier swallowing me, like I had dived into ink and could see nothing but that substance all around. I hooked my secondary safety cord to the thin metal runner that covered the ship and landed my feet on the outer hull.

The airlock closed as my bottom lip quivered and I switched on the suits arm and neck lights. They illuminated a small area around me and my eyes landed on the kill switch for the primary relay. I removed the outer case of the emergency box, inputted the command code supplied by the computer, closed my hand around the primary kill switch and pulled as I said a prayer to Jesubrahmed.

CHAPTER TWENTY TWO

FATHER'S DARKNESS

The primary kill switch plunged the ship into total darkness, internally and externally. I had a blast radius of light just eight feet wide, cast by my neck and wrist lights. The rest was total darkness. I had never been afraid of the dark, never cowered under my sheets as a child; I had known what was out there; my parents. They were in the house sitting separately while the hired help flittered around until late into the night, coming and going from rooms with the upmost discretion.

The dreams about the Panther started after I'd painted the roses and they did indeed frighten me at a young age but it wasn't the dark that scared me, it wasn't even what was in the dark, it was something else. Something I couldn't explain or understand but something that disturbed me about my parent's relationship from a young age. Sex was normal; my parents were not. As I stood in the darkness I remembered feeling this way in the house I grew up in; only ever meant to be aware of what was directly around me even though I knew there was so much more going on.

The darkness of space wasn't cold and it didn't intimidate me as I had imagined it would, instead it felt like the unflinching eyes of my father, always seeing, always judging, always pushing. Even when he was in his room planning, working or having himself dusted by the maid, it was as though he always had a presence in the house. Not one of violence or of hate but a view that anything that he disagreed with or disliked was second best; like I was second best because I was more artistic than I was scientific and so not his perfect choice of offspring; a tried and tested conventional winner.

Was I a disappointment? Not at first, when I did everything he wanted me to do perhaps better than he thought I would, but later? When I had started to paint? Almost certainly.... No, I'm certain I was a disappointment.

I looked up into that unflinching, desolate void above me and it felt hard to move. I wondered where all the stars were? I knew they were there but why could I not see them? Why was I deemed to be beneath their beauty? I knew it was a fault in me and not in the universe and yet still I could not understand why I would choose this blackness over the wonder of open space.

I commanded my legs and at first they resisted, so I looked forwards, got out my P.S.M.P (which I'd tied to my wrist just in case) and started on my quest, willing my feet to start shuffling and then finally walking. I was locked to a line of taut thick metal cord that stretched across the hull like a highway, leading to every external port, supply cache, and location that may need technical repairs. It went passed every airlock and hull locked sensor and passed all of the external ports I was looking for. I had locations and routes and my logical mind kicked into gear, willing me forward. My short cord was clipped to the four foot high tether line keeping me near the hull until I needed to change to a separate section of cord to change direction on the grid, at this point I'd attach the long cord and then take the short cord off, place it on the new section of tether and then detach the long cord once more. No-one wanted to float off into space and so this procedure had to be undertaken every one hundred yards or so as I marshalled my way around the external cargo and material pods.

Travelling along the hull, surrounded by the crushing blanket of black was stressful and the repetitive safety protocol of 'latch on, latch off, latch on, latch off' made it difficult to remain calm. A rational person like me was not easily flustered or scared and yet this feeling was so intense and familiar that I found myself on the edge of tears several times before I reached my first External port.

Standing before the dull grey external port gave me a tiny rush of achievement but that was replaced with an increased feeling of pressure. My magnetic boots locked into position and silently I was bonded to the outside of the hull. I pulled my excess cord close and stored it in my belt and then pulled off my backpack, activating the magnetic bottom so it could not float away. I placed the bag down on the hull and it was stuck fast; I was ready to begin. It had taken me over an hour to get to the port, walking straight and then around outcrops and objects and now it came down to a five minute job of re-sequencing the power coils, inputting the command code, switching off the primary grid and switching the settings to the secondary grid.

I opened the rucksack carefully and retrieved the recalibrating laser on my first time of looking for it. I sealed the bag and twisted a cord around the handle of the laser so that it couldn't be dropped or float off when I most needed it. I pointed the almost paint brush shaped laser at the hatch lock and gave it a short burst, the blue laser was detected by the sensors and the centre seal to the doors unlocked. I opened the console like I would an ancient book, the small protective doors revealing the secrets within. From this port I could alter environmental controls and energy allocation settings and yet all I really wanted was to unlock my prison; so that I could be free to roam the ship as I wished without the environmental suit on.

I set to work on the simple task of recalibration and it was simple indeed. Was I alone in thinking this was perhaps too easy a task for the safety guideline placed down by my father? Was I abnormal in my ability to remember the details of most of my lessons and training prior to the mission? I didn't think so and yet I whizzed through the task in half the time the computer had estimated it would take and so was inputting the command code listed on my P.S.M.P and then switching to the secondary grid before schedule. I checked through what I'd done to make sure I hadn't missed anything and then shut the doors to the external port. One blast of the laser locked the station again, leaving me standing before the port looking at it suspiciously. Had I done everything? Had I completed the task? I checked the notes and instructions again on my P.S.M.P and so it seemed incredibly likely that I had completed the task required of me.

I looked at the P.S.M.P's map and gathered my bearings. It had been programmed to bleep if I started heading in the wrong direction; something it was now doing. Why? I looked around and could see the tether line that went all around the hull of the ship and looked back the way I had come, realising that I would indeed have to flow back for a short while until I hooked onto another run that swung off in a different direction towards the next external port.

While still in The Buckingham I'd read the computers notes concerning the task at hand and it had clearly stated that one of the main problems I would face would be disorientation due to the size of the ship (The Buckingham was indeed massive, almost four miles wide and ten miles long, in a roughly cylindrical shape), the depth of the darkness and the disjointed nature and positioning of the externalised ports. I had considered this to be something I would not need to worry about particularly as I would know when I was going wrong and if not I would just follow my P.S.M.P, yet now that I was out on the hull I was finding it hard to trust the computer.

What if this was a layer of control and failsafe that was pre-programmed? What if I was being judged/had been judged and was now being sent out onto the hull to die so I could pose no more threat to the colonists?

It was unlikely and it was unlike me to be bewitched by such paranoid stupidity and yet I felt uneasy as I walked through the darkness, following the computers map. Pulling myself along the cord that was situated four feet off the hull I felt time distort and as I moved it felt like I was never making any real ground. The darkness still surrounded me and the computer urged me onwards into the darkness to an unseen goal, telling me I was 'closing on designated position' every two minutes, while not giving me a clear idea of how far I'd travelled unless I stopped and accessed my P.S.M.P to check. I'd stop only to find I'd gone two hundred yards in twenty minutes rather than the three miles it had felt like. My pace was erratic to say the least and I would urge myself onwards only to slip back into an amble as I watched intently for any trip hazards or large obstacles. All the while as I went I could feel the pressure, I could feel his eyes watching me, waiting for me to give him the right answer so that he could know I was 'an intellect to be cherished.'

Looking up I realised I was lighter than I had been before, somehow I was missing something obvious and it was at this point that I felt for the straps to the backpack and found they were missing; missing because I had left the bag back at the first External Port. I looked back into the darkness and my heart sank like a stone, my head dropped and a low, desperate moan passed from my lungs and out of my mouth. It was followed by a deep breath that was chased by a sob that made my whole body quake. I felt hollow as another sob quickly followed that one and then, almost like an echo building inside me, I felt an emotion rise. It built from deep in my soul and it cascaded upwards till it hit the back of my throat and burst out of me like nothing that had ever escaped before.

'WHAT THE HELL DO YOU WANT FROM ME?!' I screamed into the darkness. I screamed it like it was the most important question in the universe, and perhaps it is the most important question on every child's lips when they come of age.

'DID YOU WANT TO SEE ME FAIL?! DID YOU WANT TO SEE ME DIE OUT HERE BECAUSE I WASN'T LIKE YOU?!' The darkness watched me, its shroud of authority like an executioner's bag pulled over my eyes.

'WHY WASN'T BEING ME ENOUGH FOR YOU?! YOU COULD HAVE TOLD ME YOU WERE PROUD OF ME WHEN IT MATTERED TO ME! TO ME! WHY DID I ALWAYS HAVE TO JUMP THROUGH ONE OF YOUR DAMNED HOOPS!'

The tears came but I was not going to let that stop me now. He had always wanted so much more from me and now I was going to show him just how 'much more' I had.

'YOU WERE THE SCARED ONE! WHY DIDN'T YOU STAND UP FOR YOURSELF AGAINST HER?! FOR YOURSELF?! FOR ME?! WHY DID SHE ALWAYS WIN?! WHY DID YOU PLAY HER FUCKING GAME?!'

Silent and yet I was feeling something rise in me. A rebellion of the soul that would not be barricaded or sent to bed, that would not be patted on the head or told that I could be more if It put away childish things.

'I KNEW WHAT I WANTED TO BE FROM THAT DAY IN THE GALLERY! NO-ONE I KNOW CAN TELL ME THAT THEY KNEW... KNEW, WITHOUT ANY DOUBT, WHAT THEY WANTED TO BE AT FIVE. YEARS. OLD! I WAS DRIVEN AND VISIONARY AND GOD DAMN IT I JUST WANTED YOU TO BE PROUD OF ME FOR THAT... JUST ONE FUCKING TIME!'

Silence.

'ARE YOU LISTENING?!' I was shouting at the blackness and I no longer cared if that meant I was 'psychologically depleted'. I no longer wanted to play his game. I no longer wanted to be in control. I just wanted to be free! My face was wet with tears as I staggered to my feet, evidently that noise, that cacophony of frustration and hate, had driven me to my knees like an opposite reaction to the force I fired out into the universe.

'DO YOU EVEN CARE?! CARE?! EVEN ONE LITTLE BIT THAT I LEFT HOMEWORLD BECAUSE OF YOU AND HER?! THAT I HAD TO ESCAPE?! THAT YOU DROVE ME AWAY, AND THIS?! THIS IS ALL I HAVE LEFT FOR YOU! RAGE AND HURT AND PAIN!'

I looked at the darkness and caught something shocking, something I hadn't expected to see. I caught a glimpse of my own face in the reflection in the glass of my dome. I was puffy eyed and had my lips pulled back in anger showing my white teeth glinting in the light. My eyes were bright and my hair stuck to my face in the places where they had met my tears. I flicked my head back and I could see someone different from the woman I thought I knew looking back at me. She was passionate and angry and beautiful and I saw life in those eyes... She was the type of woman I would want to paint.

I blinked back my tears and looked down and away from the darkness to gather my thoughts. I thought of that house with the oppressive air of intellectual fascism, of how alone I had felt and how alone I felt now... Then I looked at the plates of Graphene beneath my feet. I thought of all the people contained within the shell I stood upon and how they were relying on me to switch on the power supply and maintain the ship until help arrived. I thought of the 'Indo Star', lost in space with over fifty million colonists, floating like an asteroid through the blackness, never to be awake and alive again though I always thought the colonists were still alive, locked in their sleep forever.

I thought of my muse from deck eight and the completed but un-viewed work, and deck fourteen that I hadn't finished yet and I knew I had to go back. I knew I would have to try harder to complete the task and I knew more than anything else that there was defiantly no-one up there looking down and judging me. I felt not the eyes of my father but of Jesubrahmed now upon me because I was all alone out here, and God was, and always had been, inside me.

I gathered my thoughts, feeling both my emotion coming down from a massive peak and my rational mind coming back to the fore and I was struck by an inner resolve and a perfect truth; I now knew I could, and would, complete this task. No matter how long it took or how hard it was I would make it. I started to pull myself along the Anker coil one hand after the other until I finally pulled myself through the darkness till the original external port appeared and I caught sight of the backpack still sitting locked to the hull.

When I pulled the bag on again it would stay on and I would not allow myself to put it down. Everything that came out of the bag was attached to a safety cord straight away and the bag went back on my back. I traversed the length and breathe of the ship on these Anker coils, walking through the darkness, surrounded by my 'halo' of light.

At each external port I would perform the needed task while checking my P.S.M.P and then rechecking my work. After eight hours of pulling myself along these cords I was exhausted and checked to see the final external port location. I remembered the final external port being near the tail end of the ship, meaning I was looking at another six hours in the darkness. I could have run but the increased speed would have led to increased chance of error and I didn't think it was worth it.

The task was draining, not just physically, but mentally. The feeling of danger, the knowledge that so much was riding on me getting this right was at times maddening, leading me to start talking to myself, something I tried to avoid unless I was eating with my guests or chatting with Lucile in the kitchen. The talking led to a strange new approach to the ordeal as I started to sing. There have been few times in my life when I felt like singing, even fewer when I actually have. I generally view the whole process as pointless unless you are the one being paid to sing.

Why would you try to replicate a sound you enjoy knowing you will fail, and so end up making a poor imitation that annoys others and yourself when you can't hit the notes or remember the words or completely botch the timing? Surely that would deplete the enjoyment of the song on your next listening or destroy someone else's love of it as they will recall your distorted version when they hear the music and not as it was intended.

Wasn't singing just redundant? Yet as I muttered to myself, I started to sing. Quietly, so as not to disturb anyone at first, then louder as I became more confident and happier that it was just me and so no-one else would suffer the discomfort of my botched key changes and missing words.

With each hand over hand my voice became a more dominant force in my helmet, a sound that filled my small circle of light in the great darkness. I sang what I had come to know as soft melodies and acidic verses about the breaking of a union. I then moved on to a new and sillier chapter in my journey as noises emanated from my throat, imitating the music I ran to. Beats and bangs and high pitched squeaks followed each other in strange orders and varied volumes until the final external port was reached. It appeared before me as my circle of light detected it and my heart beat faster and faster as I retrieved my tools from my bag. It was almost as though my light had winked it into existence and when I was finished it would simply disappear once more. Of course it didn't, and wouldn't, but as I recalibrated, inputted the command code and adjusted the settings, I prayed that my ordeal would finally be over.

I closed the doors and packed my bag. I was about to walk away when I saw something in the darkness, a twinkle; like a star. It was there for the briefest of seconds and then gone but it was certainly there. I knew I hadn't imagined it.

I pulled my backpack tight and checked my cord was tightly secured both to myself and then the tether coil. I looked into that darkness but nothing was there and yet I was certain I had seen it. I attached my long cord and detached my short one and let go of the coil, pushing gently away from the hull with my feet.

I fell into that darkness headfirst, my world consumed by it, devoured by the void I cast myself into. I fell until my cord pulled tight. I felt like I was suspended in nothingness and yet it did not destroy me or drive me mad, it could do no further damage to me for I was the one with a life and hope and faith and a soul and this expectant darkness was just made up of all the things that I did not understand.

It was made up of my father's need for me to prove his legacy was more than a company that fired humans into space, it was made up of what I thought was his desolation at his wife's infidelity, it was made up of his lack of emotion and his need for control... And yet it was none of those things.

I was not sure if I was travelling still or just floating in that nothingness that was made up purely of my assumptions as to how my father felt. Could it be he was like me? Controlled and yet he had come to terms with it? Could it be that he was consumed by his need to work, his want to find order in chaos and his love for others that he found hard to express? Was he a bitter man who brooded and hated? Not really.

I was inside this quagmire of discovery and emotion and burst assumption when the ship loomed back into my light bubble. I braced for the slight impact and my body bumped against the hull but my hands found the Anker coil and so I stayed there instead of yo-yoing back out into space.

Looking out into the darkness I wondered what he was really like and what he really felt? Could it be that I hurt him and he felt it deeply? That he too found his emotions exposed around me and that I had made him feel weak? I knew his attitude towards me became far more flippant and less focused after the painting.

I thought of him sitting on that sofa, looking at the painting of his wife engaging in a passionate embrace with another man, and I felt even worse thinking of the effect it must of had on him when his eyes must have swung and seen my portrayal of him as the weak, diminished rose dying in the shade behind them. For the first time ever I regretted that moment. I regretted humiliating him.

Had I compensated for that weak image I cast of him by seeing him as a control freak ever after? A man that was so guarded in his emotions that I never knew what he felt?

Had I done this to him?

I gathered my thoughts and did what I had to do. I walked. I walked back with that judging blackness above, only now it was accusing. It was morbidly hanging above me telling me how much I had hurt it and how deeply it still felt the wound.

Thoughts from my childhood clouded my mind in that darkness and when I finally found myself at the airlock I had exited originally I was exhausted and forever changed. Changed by the darkness and the truth it had revealed to me, or at least the possibility of truth that I had never considered; that I had been the original aggressor in the relationship between myself and my father and so between him and his wife. That I had forced him to face the uncomfortable reality that he was simply not enough for her.

I opened the port by the airlock and set the grid to automatically switch to the secondary relay. Once I turned the leaver I would know if this had been worth it, if I had succeeded.

My hand closed around the leaver and I prayed to Jesubrahmed to allow me this victory so that I could readdress a balance that I had disrupted, so that I could move onwards as a person; changed by my time in the shadows.

I pulled the switch and waited for the light but nothing happened. I resisted the urge to switch it off and back on again and trusted in my work, the work I had checked and double checked. I had done everything right and I knew it. So where was the power? My P.S.M.P screen clicked into life and I checked it to see the results of the power grid change and I was greeted with a loading screen that told me the computer was running a full diagnostic and system check before diverting power. I checked the time to power reinitialising and was mortified to see that it was counting down from a twelve hour clock.

I would have to wait twelve hours before the system rebooted?! Rationality took over once again and I checked my air supply, I had plenty to see me through the twelve hours and beyond but I decided it would be sensible to attach myself to the ships air system and so I would at least know I wasn't going to suffocate. I then shortened my cord so that I wouldn't float out and away from the ship and then that was it. That was all I could do.

I hung there and became aware of my power supply, checking revealed I had ninety percent of my power still intact, meaning I would be fine and yet I was convinced, irrationally, that I would see my suits power fail before the Buckingham's system's reinitialised. Facing a difficult question I allowed my rational mind to make the snap decision and so powered down everything bar the suits life support systems. As the lights went out I confess I wondered if that was the last light I would ever see. I knew I could not effect the outcome in any way now and so accepted the Universe's judgement, and that of Jesubrahmed, and soon slipped into unconsciousness.

CHAPTER TWENTY THREE

LIGHT

A distant noise pulled me back from unconsciousness, tearing me away from the void I'd disappeared into. I turned and slowly my feet found the floor and I magnetised them with a tap of the toe cap on the hull. The noise wasn't coming from my P.S.M.P but from the ship and as I looked into the darkness I was overwhelmed to see light sparkle into life along the hull. It burst forth from several portholes and finally I was bathed in it as I stood by the airlock. I looked outwards and drew a breath; the blackness was packed with points of light in all directions, so vast a number, so many pinpricks of life that I held that breath. I felt like I had cast my eyes upon beauty for the very first time. I knew that beauty had always been around me and it had always been this varied, this glorious, but now I could see it. I couldn't stop myself from letting out a scream of joy as the universe revealed itself to me as I had revealed myself to it.

I was weak, exhausted, and suffering from dehydration and a lack of food and yet that light made me feel like I was the luckiest person alive. I stepped forward and pressed the airlock release button and saw the lights flash and when the doors started opening tears formed in my eyes. I could not wipe them away and so I had to allow them their natural course of escape and was not ashamed as perhaps I would once have been when they rolled down my cheeks.

I floated into the airlock and turned around to see the systems still reinitialising in the corridors, lighting sparking into life as far as the eye could see (which for me was not far due to the tears that were replaced as soon as they left with more and more). The airlock closed and re-pressurised as I stood there, valiant and victorious and perhaps the happiest I had ever been.

I opened the inner door and stepped into the ship, closing the airlock behind me. I checked the environmental conditions were life sustaining and then eagerly cracked the seal on my suit, lifted the helmet off my head and dropped it to the floor. The air was cold and crisp and would take some time to warm but I did not care. I felt the cold on my face as I walked through the halls and passed the cryogenic pods. I waved at my muse but didn't stop, I would be back to see her later. I had the time after all.

Of course I visited the toilet, washed my hands and delighted in the cool water running over my reborn skin, and then headed for the kitchen where I grabbed the sweetest, most indulgent food I could and ate until I could take no more. I waved at my painted friends as I left to my find my bed, threw both my sleeping partners to the floor and collapsed into a deep sleep once more.

Light and stars filled my dreams and filled my heart. I was so glad to be back on board that I would not have felt negative towards The Buckingham for anything. This was my home, my sanctum, my teacher and after years of living a half life filled with regret and anger I finally found a view of the future that was full of hope. One that I knew I would make the most of.

*

It came to be the momentous day of my birthday. It was a day I had ignored for many years as I had never really seen my age, or anyone else's, as that serious a business. But then if I did think about it David's age had captivated me and the woman that I painted in Brazil was of incredible interest to me; so perhaps it was more accurate to say that MY age and birthday meant little.

This year it was different though. This year I would be marking my second birthday to pass while alone on the Buckingham. It had been months since I had reinitialised the power grid and since then everything had been working like clockwork. I even performed some repairs around the ship myself, minor ones in truth but still I took pride in knowing that the short range sensors were online, even if the long range ones were still dark.

I had been working hard in deck fourteen, and in a side room I had been developing my control of the graphene wall systems, to the point that I could program a singular wall sheet to switch into several different forms on a rotating cycle and so was displaying these 'morphic statues' in the loading bay. They were all standing waiting for the right current to bring them to life.

I programmed the walls and light emitters for several hours and then grabbed a drink and got some dinner; a roast dinner from a stasis plate with all the trimmings. It slipped down well while myself and my guests enjoyed a new thing I'd found in the databanks that I found I had learned to love; Movies.

We watched a tale of comedy and woe concerning two young lovers who found it impossible to meet and would constantly miss each other by mere seconds. It was frantic and absorbing and hilarious till the end when they felt they had missed their last chance to meet. I had practiced and worked at relaxing and allowing myself to react naturally to new stimuli and this brought me to tears of sadness when their final rendezvous was missed. They walked slowly away from each other having lost out on the happiness that they deserved only to bump into each other on the street outside the train station. The sadness turned to joy and the tears came in reaction to the happiness of union. It ended with a kiss. I wished my night would do the same yet I knew it couldn't.

I walked down to the hold that kept my statues and stood in the doorway. I waited, still holding my drink in hand, waiting for the trigger. I stepped over the threshold and the sequence I had programmed played out before me as a bright green emblazoned light fired from my position along the floor plates towards the wall. It reached the bottom of the wall opposite and climbed straight up it till it hit the ceiling and then fired back towards me. It reached the centre of the room as I stepped in, ready for the show, and it burst into a huge firework display as each explosion fired tens of small dots of light away from the detonations centre point. As these lights traced across the Graphene tiles they suddenly started exploding, sending beautiful lights across the ceiling in all the colours of the rainbow.

I sat down and watched my light show and found it beautiful. The darkness pushed away by the light of the hearts work. It was pre-programmed, but the explosions were randomised by the computer to give me surprise as well as what I knew it would contain. I loved it and once it was done the bay filled with music and I danced as the statues morphed randomly around me.

I had fun.

It would have been better with someone else there but it didn't matter really, I found I was far better company for myself nowadays; I was still me and yet slightly more relaxed, more happy. Not happy because of my solitude but in spite of it.

At one hundred you are often told your perspective may change and you find things are less important than they used to be. You didn't need to squeeze everything you can out of everyday because you know you have hundreds more in front of you. I was one hundred that night and I felt the freedom grow inside me. I felt the change and I wanted to get everything I could and more from my time. I wanted to live and live well.

On my first day of being one hundred I received a late present and one that I still smile about; I received a message.

I had taken to doing my runs at a slower pace but challenging myself in different ways. Knowing I was still being filmed constantly and that I would have to face those images I stepped out of my cabin naked bar my running shoes. I jogged around the light course with everything on show as it had been in my room hundreds of times and yet it felt different in the corridors, especially going past all those stasis locked colonists; their eyes closed as I dashed past. Did some of those heads turn? Did they wake up and find they could all remember the day the princess ran past wearing just her title?

When the unscheduled alarm chimed I stopped and warmed down on the spot and then jogged to the bridge. On the bridge the communications console was blinking like a Christmas tree and as I approached I could see it was being linked to the short range sensors. I looked at the two stations and had to sit down on Sheena's chair, the synthetic Graphene covering felt warm on my bare buttocks as I keyed in my command code and waited for the message to be opened.

Precious seconds flew as I sat sweating on that chair before the computer clicked into gear and confirmed that The Buckingham had received notification from the support vessel that it was with-in a month's range and fully prepared to complete and repairs needed. I checked and there, at the edge of the short sensors range, far away in the deepness of space, a small blip was floating.

I watched that blip for a long time before I realised what it actually meant; that I was finally going to be around people again. I was instantly hit with a wave of emotion and had to stay in that chair, riding out the mixture of fear and happiness that hit me like two asteroids impacting on a small moon. I was to be sent on my mission again, my real one.

I stood and keyed the response to be sent back to the rescue vessel; to let them know I had received their message and that I was still alive, I was still here!

In the days that followed it sank in that I had perhaps a month left before they arrived and that they would be coming in to do the repairs and then continue the mission as planned. I had completed my task; I had guarded the ship and myself from harm and survived my demons that unbeknownst to me I had readily invited on the journey with me. I was different while yet being the same as I was before. Surely I would still be slightly guarded with my emotions, probably be more cautious than most when it came to social occasions and would retain my decorum. I was new and yet could not have evolved if not for the person I had once been.

    I felt different.

CHAPTER TWENTY FOUR

THE GARDEN

One thing was left to do, something so important to me that I became obsessed with putting in as many hours as possible; I needed to finish deck fourteen.

It wasn't a wish or a like, it wasn't the kind of thing that I could simply 'let go,' and I knew on arrival they would insist on dragging me away for debriefing and assessment. I knew I needed to finish that final room, to find out what was on that final wall.

The month grew around me as the vivid hues of the new planet were almost captured by intensifying the light produced behind the paint that I placed on the outcropping walls. I had traversed all the way to the final room and on that final day of their return I heard the chimes that indicated a ship docking and I knew they would come for me. I could finish what I was doing if I just had those last few minutes to work and so instead of going to meet the ship as it docked I choked back the urge that twisted me away from that wall and I continued my work. I continued and was so close that I could feel that sense of achievement mounting in my chest. This day would be one of the greatest in my life and I was going to capture it before I answered any questions.

The brush twisted on the pallet as I dabbed the droplets of paint on the wall. In the distance I heard something I had not heard in two years, something that made my heart skip a beat and Goosebumps ripple all over my skin; the sound of someone else's voice.

I heard them and wondered what they were thinking/feeling as they approached. They were walking through as close to a direct depiction of an alien forest as they could come, the colours, textures and shapes leaping out at them as they twisted down the corridor. Then, as they walked further down the corridor, plants and flowers from Homeworld would interweave into the new and over the course of their journey into this artist's world they would come from the new to arrive surrounded by the familiar; a Homeworld garden, well maintained with painted green floors that appeared to be grass (I had programmed the floor to emit the colours themselves for practical reasons. My feet would have damaged the piece every time I entered or left it otherwise) and walls with hedges and boarders bursting with flowers; bright and alive.

In that final room they found me sitting by the wall, brush in hand. I looked around and asked them to wait and they did. They watched me quietly but I could feel their nerves and also their relief. I wanted to go to them but I needed to finish what I had started. I needed it done and so that is how we spent our time for twenty minutes.

When it was done I stepped back and left my pallet on the floor. I walked backwards and looked around at the walls that showed the bright roses that had grown at the end of the garden when I was young and free. In the centre of the room the old tree was depicted where my mother and the gardener used to entertain each other and yet now she stood alone, not sadly, but leaning with her back to the tree, her red dress the exact same hue as the red roses, light bursting through the canopy bathing her smiling upturned face. She looked happy and incredibly beautiful and as wild as any rose.

On the back wall the bushes continued around until a darker patch, the patch I had been working on. The part I knew I needed to finish. I looked at her and smiled and then turned to see David and Ben standing watching me. David had been looking at me intently and I knew he was trying to work out what exact condition I was in. Ben was nervously shuffling and his hands were clasped in front of him to stop them fidgeting.

I walked over to them and smiled a genuine, warm smile and hugged Ben. As he held me I could feel myself becoming emotional and I squeezed him as hard as I could. He held onto me tightly and I glanced at David almost to ask if it was ok, he nodded at me and smiled and looked at the walls, indicating to his surroundings as he blinked back tears of his own.

'Amazing,' he whispered and I buried my face in Bens shoulder and sobbed. That one sob wracked my body and I crumpled, Ben went with me to the floor as the next hit. It was followed by another and another and I felt like I had when space had surrounded me; as I stood on the hull, only now it wasn't an echo of anger magnifying inside my emptiness, no, this was as though I were so full that I simply had to release it.

But it wasn't anger, it was love.

I stayed with him and when those shuddering sobs gave way to tears and the tears of strain and pain shed away to joy and the inescapable knowledge that my ordeal was finally over, we talked. The three of us sat in the garden and talked. We talked about my time here on the Buckingham and how their mission had become complicated when materials ran out and more had to be mined from the Khyber Belt and that it was a mining operation my father paid for personally.

After many hours together we got up to leave and David warned me about getting used to people again and how I should try to be calm but I understood before he had even spoken his advice. I knew who I was and that I was safe. Saying that I was desperate to see people and understand them more and make connections beyond just the superficial, but I ended up taking David's advice and keeping myself level for those first few weeks.

Ben was supportive and he had been well prepared by David so he kept stupid questions to a minimum but as we went to leave he walked back to stand in front of the wall where the dark bush lay. The one I had been painting when they arrived.

I walked back and smiled at him with my vision blurred and my head so tired it felt like it was full of every night's sleep I had ever missed.

'What was so important that you needed to finish it before we could talk to you?' He asked and I hugged him and looked into the space where the panther used to stalk.

'I needed to finish it so that it was there and I could walk away,' I replied and he pulled back to look into my eyes.

'But it's just a blank wall.'

'No Ben, there's a wall and the roses.'

EPILOGE

Our colony did become known for its artistic flare and it was indeed a paradise that we respected and loved and it became home in shocking speed. Within three months we had our homes built and our lives settled on the largest continent.

There were issues with sleep disruption that we still don't fully understand and it turned out that many of the fruits that we were planning on harvesting had a hallucinogenic effect on most humans making them an unviable food source, but we worked hard and discovered others that tasted like nothing from Homeworld yet were stunning. Sweetness that made us smile and sustaining carbohydrates we could gather from the roots of other plants. It was a planet of abundance and all our needs were met by it and more.

I still live there today with my three children and loving husband. A man who knew me before and then met me after my time stranded on The Buckingham, a man who loved me for who I was and not who I had been, and accepted that who I had been was still someone special.

We laugh more now than when we first met and I love far more than I ever thought I could. There are days when I sit in the intense light, being baked from both sides by those twin suns and I smile as I watch my children scamper through the purple and orange grass that grows at the back of my house. Normally I'm sitting alone as they play, but then I leap up and throw caution to the wind and run, jump and shout with them until I simply cannot continue and so retire once more to the porch.

I live and love as much in one day as I'd want too and yet at the end of each day, before I close my eyes, my husband lies in my embrace and

I thank Jesubrahmed for allowing me to see the God within, and I know tomorrow is another day to try and be as alive as possible.

I know that I have been lucky in my life, I know I had the strongest of starts and I know I should thank my parents for their dedication in those formative years but wonder what happened to turn my mother's head so far away from my father. Was it boredom? Did she slip out of love with him, a little each day till there was nothing left, or did she just become tired of his dedication to his work? Should she have become something more than just who she was or could he have realised his work was isolating her and stepped back and tried as hard in their union as he did at work? I don't know and in all reality it makes no difference now. I make sure I try to step back from my now galaxy renowned art and just live, with the kids, with him; so we do not become them.

I am thankful of my life and my time on the Buckingham and was overjoyed when the long range communications arrays were placed between Homeworld and here so that I could speak with my parents. We talk regularly now and they still live together and though I don't know what happens behind closed doors I can imagine they are the same as they always were, but now maybe I am more accepting. I try not to judge, just let them get on with it and we are more at peace than ever in our connection.

I never did knit when I stayed on the Buckingham, though when we arrived I found an urge take me and so I created jumpers, hats, and gloves a plenty. In truth they were plain and boring when compared to the bright wonder of our new home and I was adequate at best at knitting, but I still do it today. I find it relaxing and as I drop stitches and miscount lines my mind wanders across canvas and colour and by the time I reach the end of a badly fashioned, uninspiring garment, I have an intriguing idea I want to explore completely.

My muse turned out to be nothing like how I imagined her; she didn't sound the same, move the same or even act the same. My fabrication of her fell into tatters and then was transformed into someone far more flawed and yet so much more amazing. There was also no sexual spark between us at all. We were like sisters and that pleased me immensely.

I pursued our friendship and she was only too happy to become immersed in my life as I was in hers. She met and married another wonderful man who had his papers cleared and was allowed to stay on when his time was done on The Buckingham; Ivan. They are passionate and happy and he still spends as much time as he can getting as grubby as possible but I see it more as him pursuing his interests now.

What does the future hold for this woman, one hundred and forty five years old and one of the universes most famous artists? A woman who takes a class of thirty students that show a love for art and keeps them for eighteen months in a large communal building to perfect their skill and nurture their love of art and life? A woman who is a princess, the last student of the artist Salvador Iranie, and above all else a mother and wife?

It holds whatever I want it to, whatever I work hard enough for and whatever I commit my heart to.

The Buckingham is all around me now in the structures that make up our settlements but there are four specific buildings that I love. One of them is a testing centre for Graphene based art that experiments with the material. It is constructed out of the hanger bay where I spent my one-hundredth birthday.

Two of them are galleries; one holds my exhibit from deck eight in its original composition. They removed the whole thing and replaced it panel by panel, exactly as it stood in the ship and the other holds my corridor (which has been replicated throughout the galaxy), again transported piece by piece. Finally the last is the building most precious to me.

It is my family home. If you walked inside it you would see it is incredibly clean and exceptionally cluttered with keepsakes and mementos from the past forty five years. It also has a kitchen and dining room that I spent a lot of time in while on the Buckingham. Hanging on the walls are six portraits. They share each and every meal with us.

It is my favourite room on the whole planet.

A BEGINNING

Made in the USA
Charleston, SC
09 July 2013